EARTH
FRIENDS
RIVER RESCUE

Look out for more adventures
from the Earth Friends:

FAIR FASHION

GREEN GARDEN

PET PROTECTION

EARTH FRIENDS

FRIENDS

RIVER RESCUE

HOLLY WEBB

nosy
crow

First published in the UK in 2014 by Nosy Crow Ltd
This edition published in 2021
The Crow's Nest, 14 Baden Place
Crosby Row, London, SE1 1YW
www.nosycrow.com

ISBN: 978 1 83994 019 4

Nosy Crow and associated logos are trademarks
and/or registered trademarks of Nosy Crow Ltd

Text © Holly Webb 2014
Cover and inside illustration © Owen Gildersleeve 2021

The right of Holly Webb to be identified as the author has been asserted.

A CIP catalogue record for this book is available from the British Library.

Printed and bound in the UK by Clays Ltd, Elcograf S.p.A.
Typeset by Tiger Media

Papers used by Nosy Crow are made from wood grown in
sustainable forests.

1 3 5 7 9 10 8 6 4 2

MIX
Paper from
responsible sources
FSC® C018072

www.nosycrow.com

ONE

"You look amazing." Izzy's dad laughed. "So happy, Iz! And not nervous at all."

Izzy smiled at him, and went back to staring at the newspaper. She could hardly believe that it was her in the photo. The blonde girl smiled back at her, her arms round three others. Even her glasses didn't seem too awful, Izzy noticed, amazedly. She actually looked nice.

"There should be a photo of you, too," she told her dad, putting her arm round his middle. "You were in that kitchen at school all night. You must have made at least a hundred cups of coffee."

"It was a good thing you had the refreshments, actually," her dad pointed out. "Loads of people asked me if they could give a donation for the coffee, even though it came with the ticket. You must have raised quite a lot extra that way."

"Nearly five hundred pounds," Izzy said happily. "With the tickets as well, I mean. It's loads more than we thought we'd get. I can't believe we nearly gave up a couple of weeks ago, when we thought nobody was going to come to a fashion show in a school hall."

Her dad shook his head. "I can't get over how much organising you girls did. Especially you, Izzy. Marching around on the night telling everybody what to do! I was really proud of you."

Izzy read the article again. *Fairtrade Fashion Show Success! Pupils at Park Road School organised a fabulous evening of fashion and dance this Tuesday, raising money for a Fairtrade clothing cooperative in Bangladesh. The show was inspired by a school project on Fairtrade, and the funds will go towards a new school building for the cooperative.*

They had done so well. Tara was going to send the money through today, she'd said. She'd already emailed the people who ran the cooperative, telling them all about the girls, and sending them some photos of the show. She'd forwarded Izzy and Poppy and Maya and Emily the reply she'd had, with some photos of the children who would use the school, and messages from them. They'd been so happy and excited that their school was getting closer to being built. Izzy had stuck one of the photos up in her room.

"You should send a copy of this to your mum," her dad suggested quietly.

Izzy swallowed.

"I bought five copies. We can spare her one, Iz."

Izzy nodded. "I suppose so." She hadn't even told her mum about the fashion show, she realised. She hadn't spoken to her in ages, and then it had only been a quick phone call. No time to explain everything that was going on. "Do you think she'll want it?" she asked doubtfully.

"Of course she will!" Her dad sandwiched her close. "She will be incredibly proud of you, just like I am."

Izzy nodded, as much as she could squashed up against his scratchy wool jumper. But she wasn't totally convinced. Her mum lived so far away now, and the time difference with Australia made phoning tricky. Plus whenever she called, she felt like she might wake up Jack, her new half-brother. Or her mum. She was always saying how tired she was.

She sighed, very quietly, so her dad didn't hear. He was trying really hard to do everything, so that she didn't miss her mum too much. But looking at the photos just made Izzy wish her mum had been there, so she'd actually seen how amazing it had been. She didn't want to have to *tell* her. There was a photo of Maya and her mum underneath the one of all of them. Maya would probably be really annoyed about that, Izzy thought, smiling. She didn't like being known as the daughter of a famous singer. She'd only told Izzy and the others about it a week or so ago, when the fashion show had looked as though it wasn't going to get off the ground. They'd been desperate to get some more publicity, and getting the amazing India Kell to say what a brilliant idea she thought it was had worked perfectly. But it had meant that Maya's secret was out.

Maybe everybody had mum-issues, Izzy thought sadly. Still, at least Maya's mum was *there*, or most of the time she was. For the important things, anyway. Izzy hadn't seen her mum since Christmas.

Her dad was still looking at the photo, and then back at Izzy, with a slightly worried expression on his face. "Iz, did you have make-up on in this picture?"

Izzy grinned. "Yes, Dad." Sometimes he thought she was still about six. Clothes and things were not really his strong point, which was why he'd volunteered to do the coffees and teas for the show.

"I didn't even know you had any!" Her dad stared at her, as though she was some strange alien species. A *Girl*…

"I've got a couple of lipglosses, but not much. That wasn't my make-up. It was Leah, Tara's daughter. Remember? Tara from the Fairtrade shop that lent us all the clothes to do the show? Leah organised the models from her sixth-form college, for the women's clothes. She said we all had to wear some make-up, even if we were only backstage, in case we had to go on and sort out things. And to make us all feel like we were in a costume, and part of the show. She must have done it on purpose, actually, because she and her mum had it planned that we were all going to go on-stage at the end."

Her dad nodded helplessly. He still looked worried. He hated shopping for clothes, although he did his best, and made a real effort to take her to the shopping centre sometimes. But Izzy knew he worried about her getting older, and needing her mum, or somebody at least, to help her with girly stuff.

"Don't worry, Dad!" she said suddenly, flinging her arms round his waist.

He looked down at her in surprise – Izzy wasn't always a huggy person. Usually he hugged her, not the other way round.

"I miss Mum, of course I do. But I don't miss out on stuff. I don't need Mum to show me how to use make-up and things. It's all right."

"Are you sure?" her dad muttered. "I know you love science, and maths, and the kind of things I like talking about, but sometimes I worry that you're not getting a chance for the arty stuff your mum was so good at. And I certainly don't have a clue about make-up. I couldn't tell you what the difference between lipgloss and – and lip polish was."

"Nail polish, Dad. Even I know that."

"There you are, you see!" He sighed. "Neither of us is an expert, Iz. I don't want you missing out." He stroked her hair, staring at her anxiously. "At least you've got your friends at school to help. I really liked them. Especially Poppy – she was a great help at the washing up, she did loads, didn't complain once."

Izzy smiled. It was true. Poppy had washed mountains of mugs, and Izzy had dried them all up, while they chatted about their amazing evening.

Then her smile drooped a little. It was so sad that the show was over. And tomorrow was their last lesson working on the Fairtrade project. After that, everything would be different.

"Mr Finlay says we can run the sheets through the laminator after we've stuck everything in," Emily explained. "Then we can punch holes in, and string them into a book. He says that'll make it last longer than sticking it on to a poster." She smiled proudly. "I think he wants to be able to show it off to people."

Poppy sighed. "I just can't believe the show's over. Yesterday I was still on a bit of a high because it was only the night before, but now I feel really sad that we won't be doing it again."

Maya nodded. "I know. It was so special."

"But don't you get to do cool stuff like that all the time?" Emily asked. "I mean, your mum does concerts still, doesn't she? Don't you get to go backstage and be a VIP?"

Maya shrugged. "Sometimes. But it's actually a bit boring. Everyone's rushing around, and I end up just sitting in her dressing room. It's cool standing on the side of the stage when she's actually singing – there's a really good vibe then, and everyone feels special. But I don't have an important part in it, like we all did on Tuesday." She smiled, remembering. "And it was really nice being the person that mattered for once." She made a face. "That sounds really mean, but when the newspaper people were asking us about how we came up with the idea, and whether it had been hard to organise – it was actually us they were interested in. Not just because we were someone's daughters."

"*I* wouldn't mind hanging around concerts," Emily pointed out. "But I know what you mean."

"We ought to get on with sticking all our stuff in," Izzy pointed out. "We've only got till lunch."

"And there's loads of it," Maya agreed. "Come on then."

They were still frantically sticking down sheets of notes, and the photos they'd printed out, when suddenly an edgy whisper ran round the class.

"It's Mrs Angel," Emily muttered, looking anxious. Her two younger brothers had a habit of getting into trouble, and the head teacher seemed to think that Emily was a troublemaker too, even though she was nothing like Toby and James.

"You've not done anything," Izzy said, trying to sound comforting. "Don't worry."

Emily nodded nervously. "She just always makes me feel I've done something awful."

"Well, she makes me feel like that too, and she's

never even told me off." Izzy shrugged. "It's a head teacher thing. I bet she's done a course in it."

Emily sniggered, then wiped the smile off her face as Mrs Angel stopped talking to Mr Finlay and stared in their direction. "Oh no, she *is* coming to say that Toby and James have broken something!"

"Good morning, everyone!"

The girls exchanged relieved glances. That was definitely Mrs Angel's end of term prizegiving voice, not the telling-off one. They were in the clear.

"I've got some exciting news." Mrs Angel was smiling now, a big toothy proud head-teacher smile. She looked a bit like a peckish shark. Izzy tried not to giggle. The peckish shark was still eyeing their table.

"I'm sure you all signed the petition that Izzy, Poppy, Emily and Maya organised, asking for the school to change to a Fairtrade cotton jumper."

"I didn't," Ali muttered from the table behind them, and Izzy and the others all turned round to glare at her.

"Honestly, she's such a little pain in the neck," Emily growled. "It's a good cause, and she has to be stupid about it, just because it was our idea."

Maya rolled her eyes. "Well, don't sound like

you're surprised."

"The governors told me that they would like to change to a Fairtrade uniform, girls, and we've gone through all the costings now – so I can confirm we will be switching jumpers. Your petition worked! Well done!"

"Wow…" Izzy murmured, her eyes widening. She'd thought that Mrs Angel was going to tell them it was all too expensive or something like that. She hadn't realised they'd actually done it!

"The chairman of the governors told me that they were so impressed with the way you organised your fashion show, girls, and the response from the rest of the school, and the parents. They said that you'd clearly tapped into strong feelings in the local community."

"Did we?" Emily whispered, looking a bit surprised.

Izzy tried very hard not to laugh.

"Mrs Brooker tells me that we're running short on our stock of school sweaters, so she'll be making a new order soon, from one of the Fairtrade manufacturers you found for us."

"Do you realise that everyone who comes to our school, for *years*, is going to be wearing a Fairtrade jumper, because of us?" Maya murmured, sounding a bit shocked at the idea.

"We're fabulous," Emily said happily.

Izzy beamed. The show had been amazing, and this was like the icing on the cake. She just felt so happy, better than she had in ages.

"Are you finished with your scrapbook, girls?" Mr Finlay asked, eyeing the pile of sheets and looking pleased.

Izzy nodded. "I think this is everything." Her all-important List that they'd used to plan the fashion show had been given a page to itself. The others had said they had to. "It saved our skin," Maya had said firmly, sticking down a neatly lettered label at the top. IZZY'S LIST.

"Looks excellent. All right, everyone! Let's clear the scissors and things away. I'll put the posters up after school. Project's finished!"

"Great," Izzy heard Ali's friend Elspeth muttering. "Most boring project ever."

Ali crammed a handful of scissors into their tray. "I know, I can't wait to get back to normal."

The smile faded from Izzy's face. Back to normal.

No more sitting with Poppy and Maya and Emily. The smile came back, a bit twisted, just for a second. It seemed funny that she was actually going to miss

Emily. They hadn't got on at all at the start of the project, when Maya had suggested Izzy worked with her group. Emily had been really stroppy about it.

Her usual table was at the other side of the room, with Lara and Sophy, who were each other's best friends. They were perfectly nice to Izzy, but all they did was giggle all the time, and draw pictures of horses. They were both pony-obsessed. The other day they'd asked Izzy, quite seriously, whether if she had to be a pony, she'd rather be a chestnut or a grey? Izzy had muttered grey, but she was thinking about those scary aliens with the oval eyes that were supposed to have landed in the desert in America somewhere. She'd rather have an alien than a pony. And she'd rather do anything than go back to sitting with Lara and Sophy again. Because they'd been working on their projects so much, she'd ended up sitting with Poppy and the others almost all the time over the last couple of weeks – it was just easier that way. But now she didn't have an excuse for that any more. She'd have to go back to her old table, and smile at stupid ponies.

The excitement about their amazing success died away. Izzy grabbed a handful of paper scraps, squishing them together, and went to put them in the recycling. That way she could sniff without anybody noticing.

"Are you missing the show again?" Poppy asked her sympathetically as she came back. "You looked really miserable for a minute!"

Izzy nodded. "It's a let-down, isn't it?" she whispered, wondering if her eyes were red. Ali and Lucy and Elspeth had told her she looked like a white rabbit once, the kind that had scarlet eyes. Izzy quite liked rabbits, but she knew they hadn't meant it as a compliment.

"At least it's swimming this afternoon," Poppy pointed out. "That'll cheer you up. Want to sit next to me on the coach?"

Izzy nodded gratefully. She did like swimming.

And then tomorrow morning, she'd be back in Ponyland…

TWO

Izzy climbed out of her dad's truck slowly, and gave him a wave. For the first time in a fortnight, she wasn't looking forward to going to school.

She trudged along the pavement, eyeing the playground through the railings. She could see Ali and Elspeth and Lucy squashed up on one of the benches, reading a magazine. Ali glanced up, and caught Izzy looking at them. She said something to the other two, and they all laughed meanly.

Izzy turned scarlet, and hurried in through the gate, and over to the other side of the playground. Now that she was back sitting with Lara and Sophy, Ali would start picking on her again, she knew. Their table was next to Lara and Sophy's and those two wouldn't stick up for her. They probably wouldn't even notice, not unless Ali turned into a Shetland pony.

RIVER RESCUE

She could see Poppy, sitting on the grassy bank close to the door to the Juniors. She was watching butterflies, Izzy realised, after a minute of trying to work out why Poppy kept bobbing this way and that. Izzy wished she could go and sit with her, but the project was over now. Poppy wouldn't want her. She hurried past with her head down, not noticing that Poppy waved. She went and sat on the steps, pulling a book out of her bag. She'd started making sure she always had a book in her bag after a couple of weeks in Year Four – the year when everything seemed to go wrong. It was the year her best friend Daisy moved house and had to go to a different school, and the year that Mum married her new boyfriend, and went from being not in the house, which was horrible, to not even in the country, which was disastrous.

It hadn't taken Izzy long to work out that a book was a good disguise. Even if you didn't actually want to read it, a book made you look as though you were doing something. Instead of standing around desperately wishing someone would talk to you. Or that you were brave enough to go and talk to them. If someone (probably Ali or Lucy) said something mean to you, you could hide behind a book if you were crying. And people tended to leave you alone if

15

they thought you were busy. Teachers on playground duty weren't as likely to try and push her into a game. With a book, she could just melt into the background.

After a while, she actually started reading the books, too.

"Izzy, have I done something to make you mad with me?"

Izzy looked up, shocked. She had a book. She was sitting in an out of the way corner of the playground. No one was supposed to talk to her.

Poppy was standing in front of her looking anxious, with Emily and Maya hovering behind at the sort of distance where they could come and back her up, but they weren't getting in the way.

"No! Of course not..." Izzy looked horrified. "Why would you think that?"

"Well, you walked straight past me this morning. And then you went back to sitting with Lara and Sophy, instead of with us."

Izzy opened and shut her mouth a couple of times. She didn't seem to be able to get words out. "But that's what I thought you'd want..." she murmured at last, looking up at Poppy unhappily. "It isn't our Fairtrade project any more. I was only sitting with you for that – because Maya asked if I wanted to."

"And you didn't really?" Poppy asked sadly. "I know you asked Mr Finlay if you could work on your own. Didn't you like being with us?"

"Of course I did!" Izzy almost shouted. How could Poppy think she hadn't enjoyed it? "It was brilliant, but you and Emily and Maya are – I mean, you're proper friends. I didn't think I could keep hanging around with you now."

Poppy sat down next to her on the little bit of wall. There wasn't much room. "Has Emily been mean to you again?" she asked suspiciously, glancing over at Emily and Maya.

"Nope. She's actually been really nice, the last few days." Izzy tried not to sigh.

"So why don't you want to be friends with us now?"

"B-but I do…" Izzy stammered. "I just didn't think I could. You were only putting up with me."

Poppy looked at her, and shook her head. "You're such an idiot," she said, but nicely. "It's probably to do with your star sign. Were you born in September? Or the end of August?"

Izzy nodded slowly. "The first of September. How did you know that?"

Poppy shrugged, but there was a smug look on her

face, as she counted off her points on her fingers. "Very hard-working. Nervous about friendships, and not very confident. But very clever. You really had to be a Virgo."

"I'm not sure I believe in all that stars stuff," Izzy said apologetically, hoping Poppy wouldn't mind. She just couldn't pretend she believed in it.

Poppy shrugged. "I do and I don't. Sometimes it works, but sometimes things don't fit at all. Virgos aren't really supposed to be great organisers, so that obviously doesn't work."

Izzy turned pink at the compliment, and Poppy hauled her up off the step. "Come on. Let's all go and sit on the bank." It was everyone's favourite part of the playground, the grassy slope that ran around the edge of the main playground and up to the field that they used for PE.

"Do you think Mr Finlay will let me change places, and come and sit with you?" Izzy asked, rather shyly. She still wasn't sure what Maya and Emily felt about her moving. She suspected it was Poppy's idea.

"I shouldn't think he'd mind," Maya said, stretching her feet out in front of her, and sighing happily. It was sunny, for the first day in ages, and she wanted her legs to get brown. "Just warn me if any of the teachers are coming. I don't want a lecture on sun cream, it's no way hot enough to burn."

"Mr Finlay got all the parents telling him how fabulous he was after the fashion show – and he's Mrs Angel's favourite person now," Emily pointed out. "He oughtn't to complain! It would be totally unfair if he did!"

"I think we shouldn't ask," Poppy suggested. "Is he going to notice?"

"He might not, but I bet Miss Grace will." Emily lay down on the grass. "She notices everything."

Poppy sighed, rolling on to her stomach next to Maya. "I hadn't thought of her. All right, we'll have to ask properly then. We'll do it after break. Mr Finlay's always in a better mood when he's had a cup of tea."

Izzy sucked in a nervous breath, and Poppy looked up at her, squinting against the sun. "What's the matter? He won't mind, Izzy. He said we worked together really well."

"It isn't him," Izzy muttered, staring at the grass as though she'd seen a legion of spiders marching through it. "It's Ali. And Lucy and Elspeth. Coming this way."

Poppy turned over and sat up in seconds, glaring.

Izzy had told them a bit about the way Ali had treated her, and even just Izzy's face as she described the things they'd said to her had made Poppy furious. "If they so much as try to be mean to you, we'll tell Mrs Angel. I mean it," she added fiercely.

"It's all right," Izzy said, trying to sound firm. "I'm not scared of her."

Maya was sitting up now too. "Aren't you? I am." She nudged Izzy. "She's a slug. A big, slimy slug, with expensive hair clips." She nodded encouragingly. "What is she?"

"A slug." Izzy managed a small grin. "In sunglasses."

"Mmm, let's hope they get taken off her," Emily said, looking at Ali's pink sunglasses enviously. "There was a letter home, wasn't there? We aren't allowed them."

Maya sighed. "Unless you've got medical reasons. Guess who's got *fragile eyes*."

Emily snorted. "She hasn't! She's got a mum she walks all over, that's all. What do you want?" she snapped at Ali and the other two, who were now standing next to them. Ali was smiling sweetly.

"We just came to talk to Maya," she purred. "Is that OK, Emily?"

Emily scowled, but she couldn't really tell Ali she

wasn't allowed to talk to Maya, however much she'd like to.

Maya was fidgeting on the grass, wishing that Ali would just say whatever mean thing it was she was going to say, and go.

"We came to say thank you." Ali smiled in a sickly sort of way.

All four of the other girls stared up at her suspiciously.

"For the fashion show. It was your idea, wasn't it, Maya?" Ali sat down next to Maya, still smiling.

Maya nodded, and tried hard not to edge away from Ali. She was known for her meanness, and she was remarkably good at saying horrible things with the sweetest smile, which made them seem even nastier.

"It was a brilliant idea. And you all organised it so well." Ali smiled round at them all.

"Who does she think she is, the Queen?" Emily muttered to Izzy, and Izzy had to stifle a snort. Emily was right. Ali had that look of her gracious majesty, talking to her loyal subjects. She just needed a corgi, and a big flowery hat.

"We really loved the modelling," Elspeth put in, smiling in exactly the same way Ali had.

"And the chance to meet your mum, Maya," Lucy added. A sudden twitch ran through all the girls, as though someone had flicked a switch.

Izzy eyed Ali sideways. She'd gone a little bit pink, and it wasn't just the sun. So that was what it was all about. That was why they were buttering Maya up.

"She's so cool." Ali's smile went up several notches. "You're so lucky having a pop star mum."

"She isn't really a pop star," Maya muttered. "She doesn't do much pop stuff any more." She looked incredibly uncomfortable, and Izzy remembered her saying how much she hated people going on about her mum – it was why she'd moved schools to Park Road, because everyone at her posh girls' school made such a fuss about it.

Ali shrugged. "She's a star, anyway."

"Yes, she is," Maya said firmly. She sounded as though she thought Ali was leading up to some snide comment about her mum's singing. But Ali just kept on smiling, while Maya and the others fidgeted uncomfortably.

How can she be so sure of herself? Izzy wondered. *Can't she see that we're all wishing they'd go away and leave us alone?* But Ali didn't seem to be able to think about herself like that. She *knew* everybody loved her. Or if they didn't, it was their loss.

Izzy watched her enviously. They must be the two most different people in the world. Still, she wouldn't want to be mean and nasty, so maybe she was better off the way she was.

"Oh, the bell!" Maya said gratefully, jumping up as it rang. "Er, I need the loo. See you in class."

"Me too!" Emily muttered, and Izzy and Poppy agreed, hurrying off after Maya.

"What was all that about?" Emily muttered as they walked as fast as they possibly could without actually running down the corridor. Mrs Angel had spies.

"It's happening all over again, just like my old school," Maya said bitterly, shoving open the door of the girls' loos.

"Excuse me? Are we sucking up to you, Miss daughter of a pop star?" Poppy elbowed Maya in the ribs. "Take that scowl off your face, you look like you're sucking a lemon."

Maya looked round at her in surprise, and then laughed. "OK. Sorry. I just really hate it…"

"That's OK, we all hated Ali already anyway," Izzy pointed out quietly. "It isn't as if she's changed. We're just adding 'totally two-faced' to her description, that's all. She's a two-faced horrible slug."

"Don't underestimate her." Emily shook her head. "At least three faces. Maybe even four."

"I wish I knew how she does it." Izzy glanced round them all, hoping she was going to be able to explain what she meant. "Couldn't she see we all wanted her to get lost, but we weren't rude enough to say it?"

Maya shrugged. "It's because she's got everyone scared. We all tiptoe round her because we think she's about to explode into something horrible. I was waiting for the bomb to drop, and it never did."

Izzy sighed. "I wish I could be just a tiny bit like her, though."

The others stared at her, and Poppy put her head on one side, as though she was examining some weird creature she'd found under a rock.

"Just the nerve!" Izzy added. "Not the rest of her. She's so brave." She frowned. "No. Not brave. It's that she just can't see that anyone could possibly not want her to be their friend. Like if she offers, everyone's going to jump at it."

Poppy shrugged. "Most of our class probably would. Just because they'd be scared of what she might do if they said no."

"But it's as if she thinks we'll all forget the horrible

stuff she's said before! She was even being nice to *me*!"

Emily stared at her thoughtfully. "And if she kept on doing it, I bet you'd go along with it. She's one of those people. She's always been like it, ever since reception, hasn't she?"

Izzy nodded. "Mmm. I suppose so. I wouldn't be friends with her, though." She shivered. "I really hope I wouldn't, anyway."

"Does anyone actually need the loo?" Maya asked. "We're going to get in massive trouble if we don't hurry up. And we want to ask Mr Finlay about Izzy sitting with us, remember."

They barged for the door, and speed-walked along to the classroom, arriving at the door just before Mr Finlay did.

Emily pushed Izzy to the front, and they all smiled at him hopefully, except for Izzy, who went bright scarlet and stared at the floor until Poppy poked her in the back. "Izzy wants to ask something."

Izzy swallowed. "Please could I move to sit with Poppy and Maya and Emily?" she gabbled.

"I didn't catch a word of that, but if you were asking if you could move tables, yes. I was going to ask you if you wanted to. Providing you don't mess around." Mr Finlay glared at them, mock-sternly.

"We won't!" Poppy promised, grabbing Izzy and steering her into the classroom, and the others nodded, all trying to look saintly.

"As if we mess around," Emily hissed indignantly, back at their table. "Well. Hardly ever, anyway."

◆

Izzy and Poppy had both brought lunches from home, so they were sitting together in the dining hall, waiting for Emily and Maya to come back from the lunch queue.

"I can't believe you thought we didn't want you sitting with us," Poppy told Izzy.

Izzy shrugged uncomfortably. It was hard to explain without sounding even more stupid. She just wasn't used to people actually liking her any more. "I suppose I'm just used to being mostly on my own," she said, going red again. She could feel her cheeks burning. That was such a feeble thing to say. She stared at her sandwiches (Dad had gone mad, there looked like half a cucumber in there).

"Well, you shouldn't be," Poppy said firmly. "Being on your own's fine sometimes, but it can be bad for your inner harmony."

"My what?" Izzy stopped trying to decucumberise

her sandwich and looked up at Poppy.

Poppy sighed. "You really don't know anything about alternative therapies, do you?"

Izzy shook her head. "I did go to a yoga class once," she offered, and Poppy looked hopeful for a second. "But I hated it," she added. "They talked a bit about harmony and stuff, but it was mostly just sitting around with your legs in the air. It felt stupid."

Poppy shook her head. "OK. Inner harmony just means not being miserable anyway. All I mean is, being on your own all the time makes you fed up."

Izzy shrugged. "I know. But trying not to be on your own and then getting told to go away because you're boring makes you feel even worse."

"Who said that?" Poppy asked indignantly.

"Most of the girls in our class," Izzy sighed. "I'm sort of marked, I think. As the boring one."

"But you aren't!" Poppy argued. "You're funny. And you have brilliant ideas. We couldn't have organised all the stuff for the fashion show without you."

"Mmm, I'm *organised*. Being organised is so exciting." Izzy grinned at her shyly.

"Yeah, OK, I see what you mean. But you are funny. See? What you just said was funny."

"Maybe." Izzy nodded.

"Is your dad picking you up today?" Poppy asked suddenly.

Izzy nodded. "Yes. He always does." Izzy's dad was a gardener, and he fitted his work in around school hours. It usually worked, although she did have to go to work with him in the holidays now that her mum wasn't there. She usually sat in his truck with a book unless there was something she could help with. "Almost always, anyway. I go to after-school club if he's got a big job on."

"Do you think he'd let you come over to mine?" Poppy said hopefully. "My mum wouldn't mind. She only works mornings on Fridays, so she'd be picking me up."

Izzy swallowed, suddenly nervous. She'd met Poppy's mum when she'd taken all the girls to Tara's clothes shop to find out about Fairtrade clothes. She was really nice – friendly and funny.

But she hadn't been over to a friend's house all this year. Not for most of last year either actually. How sad was that.

"Would your dad let you?" Poppy asked anxiously. "Would he say it was too short notice?"

"I don't think so…" Izzy said slowly. She knew her

dad wouldn't mind at all. He was more likely to give Poppy's mum a hug, to be honest. She knew how much it upset him that she was lonely. That was why he kept signing her up for stuff like yoga, and ballet (even more of a disaster, Izzy was not made for ballet). She smiled at Poppy. "He really likes you – he said you were good at washing up. He likes people who get on with stuff and don't whinge about working."

Poppy sighed. "I'm fabulous at washing up. My mum thinks dishwashers use too much energy, she's trying to make us more eco-minded and save money at the same time. She says she's got three dishwashers – me, Jake and Alex – and she doesn't see why she should buy another one." She looked at Izzy hopefully. "So would you like to come over? Will you ask him?"

Izzy nodded. She still didn't quite believe what was happening. Poppy had that look now – that slightly worried look that meant she wasn't sure if someone might laugh at her. "I'd really like to," Izzy murmured. "I'll definitely ask him."

"Good." Poppy beamed at her, and the others came back with their lunches – baked potatoes and salad.

"Whatever the veggie option was, it looked like

glue," Maya explained.

"Hey, Maya!" Ali walked past their table with Elspeth and Lucy trailing behind her, and Maya half-smiled. Luckily, the lunch tables only had room for six at the most, otherwise Ali looked like she would have tried to sit with them.

"This is going to drive me mad," Maya wailed, as soon as they were out of earshot on the other side of the dining hall.

"She doesn't take a hint, does she?" Emily muttered. "They're still all staring at you, by the way."

"Aaaargh!" Maya moaned. "Why can't I just have a normal mum like everybody else?"

Izzy tried not to drop her sandwich. Maya had no idea she was being tactless – she'd only joined the school that year, and she didn't know that Izzy's mum and dad were divorced, and Izzy hardly saw her any more.

"Ow!" Maya stared at Poppy in surprise. "What was that for?"

Poppy had kicked her under the table, Izzy realised.

Poppy sighed. "Maya! I was trying to tell you, tactfully, that not everyone's mum is normal. Actually mine's a monster half the time," she added jokily, but she was looking at Izzy sideways, obviously worried.

"It's OK. My mum lives in Australia. She got married again, and I've got a baby brother," Izzy explained to Maya. "You weren't supposed to know all that, don't worry."

"Oh." Maya looked guilty. "I wouldn't have said it if I had known, Izzy."

"It's really OK. I'm sort of used to not seeing her," Izzy lied. "What are we going to do about Ali?" she said quickly. Even though she was upset, she still enjoyed saying "we" like that, feeling part of a special group again. It was great.

"We could just try telling her to get lost," Emily suggested. "It would be simple."

"She'd kill us," Poppy pointed out.

"I wouldn't." Izzy shivered. "You don't know how mean she can be. Really, deliberately on-purpose cruel. And she's clever about it," she added. "It isn't just pushing you over in the playground, or anything like that." Her eyes were burning with tears, just thinking about it. "She told Mrs Gratton I had nits last year. I got sent home. My dad was furious, he even came in and saw Mrs Angel and said they were bullying me, but Ali said she'd just made a mistake. She apologised really nicely. And then the next day she told the whole class."

Emily made a face. "I remember now. But you did have…" She trailed off as Izzy looked up at her furiously. "OK, I'm guessing you didn't."

"It was ants!" Izzy hissed. "She'd brought them into school, and she threw them at me, and then she told everyone. She said it was because I told on her."

"She put ants in your hair?" Maya asked, horrified.

"Yeah, like I said, she's clever," Izzy said miserably. "Don't get on her bad side. If you can help it."

"Are you planning your next mission, girls?"

They all jumped, and Maya nearly tipped her lunch over.

"Sorry!" Mr Finlay moved Emily's cup, so she didn't spill it. "I didn't mean to creep up on you. You were all looking so serious, I wondered if you'd come up with another project."

"Um, not yet…" Emily said slowly. "Do you think we should, Mr Finlay?"

"Definitely! I still haven't got over the last one, mind you." He grinned. "But seriously, girls, you worked together so well. Why not?"

They nodded thoughtfully.

"Although it probably wouldn't be popular with Mrs Angel if you picked another school policy to fight against," Mr Finlay pointed out hurriedly. "I think the Fairtrade jumper was enough for the minute."

"So we shouldn't campaign for longer summer holidays then?" Poppy sighed.

"Better not. But have a think, girls. I'll be interested to see what you come up with."

He really meant it, Izzy thought, as he walked away. She just wished she could think of something that they could do...

THREE

"Dad, you remember Poppy from the fashion show?" Izzy looked at him pleadingly. *Please don't have anything planned!* she said to herself hopefully. Occasionally they went to the cinema on Fridays, or drove to visit her grandma.

"Yes, I do!" Her dad beamed at Poppy. "The champion mug-washer-upper."

"That's me." Poppy smiled back. "Please, can Izzy come back to my house tonight? And stay for tea?"

Izzy watched her dad's eyes widen, and a delighted smile spread across his face. "Of course…" he started to say, and then he trailed off, and looked at her worriedly. Oh no – he had arranged to go and see Gran, after all.

But that wasn't it. "Izzy, you do want to go?" He sounded anxious, and Izzy stared back at him in surprise. Of course she wanted to go! Why wouldn't she?

Oh! Of course – he was thinking of Ali, and the way she'd lied. He wasn't sure if Poppy wasn't pressuring her to come over. Izzy hugged him. "It's OK, Dad, really. Poppy isn't like that at all."

Poppy stood there looking confused, and Izzy's dad glanced at her apologetically. "I'm sorry, Poppy. Izzy had some trouble with one of the other girls in your class – I was just checking…"

Poppy nodded. "I've been on Ali's bad side too," she assured him.

Izzy's dad sighed. "I don't understand girls sometimes," he muttered. "Is she just horrible to everybody?"

Poppy and Izzy looked at each other, and nodded. "Pretty much," Izzy agreed.

Poppy's mum walked over, smiling hopefully. "Is it OK for Izzy to come round? Poppy really enjoyed getting to know her better when we did our trip to that lovely clothes shop."

"It's very nice of you to have her. I'll give you my phone number. Shall I take your stuff home with me now, Izzy? Gives us less chance to forget it later." He sorted out the numbers with Poppy's mum, and

gave Izzy a kiss, then headed off to his truck with her school bag, waving.

"Don't forget, Poppy, you promised to take Billy for a walk this afternoon," Poppy's mum reminded her as they walked down the road to the car.

Poppy made a face. "I haven't taken him on a really long walk in ages. Do you mind coming out for a walk, Izzy? I'd forgotten."

Izzy shook her head, smiling shyly. "Is Billy a dog? I'd love to go for a walk."

"He's an English Bull Terrier. He's gorgeous, and ever so friendly, not scary at all. But he's really dim. Totally stupid. Alex calls him the dumb blond, because he's a sort of reddish-gold colour."

Izzy laughed. "Bull Terriers are supposed to be so fierce, though, aren't they?"

Poppy shrugged. "Whoever said that didn't tell Billy. He's a sweetheart. But they have a bad reputation. We got Billy from a shelter, his last owners didn't want him because he'd got too big."

Izzy frowned. "But what did they think was going to happen? Puppies grow up."

"Exactly!" Poppy nodded approvingly.

"What Poppy isn't telling you is that Billy is pretty enormous, even for a Bull Terrier," Poppy's mum put in. "He's got a chest like a barrel. And he's incredibly strong."

Poppy started to laugh. "Not long after we got him, I answered the door, and it was a man trying to get Mum to buy double glazing. I kept saying we didn't want any, and that Mum and Dad were both busy, and he just wouldn't go away. Billy had come to the door as well, and he happened to see next door's cat walk along our front wall, just as the double glazing man was getting really annoying. He kept calling me Miss in a really nasty sort of voice." She chuckled to herself.

"What did you do?" Izzy asked, intrigued.

"It was very naughty," Poppy's mum said, but she didn't sound as though she minded all that much.

"I let go of Billy's collar." Poppy grinned. "And he'd seen Pepper from next door, so he went off like a rocket. He's not bright, like we said, and he's got a sort of one-track mind. If he wants something, he just goes and gets it, unless you tell him not to. So he went to bark his head off at Pepper – straight through the double glazing man. He only knocked the man into the hedge," she told Izzy reassuringly. "He wasn't hurt."

"But he could have been, and he was very, very

cross," her mum reminded her. "Still, he should have known to take no for an answer." She smiled at the girls in the rear-view mirror. "Strangely enough, no one's tried to come and sell us anything at the door since. I think we're on a blacklist."

Poppy sniggered.

"Is it OK for us to take Billy for a walk?" Izzy asked, a little anxiously. "When he's so big, I mean?"

"It's all right. He's pretty good. We don't usually let him off the lead – he might not come back if he saw something more interesting, and he's got no road-sense at all, either. But if he's on the lead, he walks fine. He's got one of those extending leads," Poppy explained. "We just have to hold on tight if there's a cat."

"Or a squirrel," her mum added.

"Oh yeah. Or a dustbin lorry, he really doesn't like those."

"Why not?" Izzy asked, her eyes widening. This was a whole new world – she'd never had a dog, her mum didn't like them, and Dad said it wouldn't be fair now with them both out all day. Izzy had tried arguing that a dog could go to work with him, but he wasn't convinced.

Poppy shook her head. "I'm not sure. The smell?

38

Or maybe he doesn't like the way the bins go up and down at the back. He barks his head off, and tries to chase them. It's really embarrassing. We had to give our dustmen some chocolates at Christmas after he slipped out of the gate one morning and chased them all down the road." She shuddered, remembering. "He wasn't quite as big then, luckily. And one of the dustmen had a Bull Terrier too, he was really nice about it. His one goes ballistic at fire engines, he said."

Izzy decided that she wasn't going to offer to hold Billy's lead, as there was bound to be a dustbin lorry rolling past just at the wrong moment, and she wasn't sure she could face grovelling to a team of angry dustmen.

She could hear excited barking as they walked up the path to Poppy's house, and somebody shouting from indoors. It sounded like, "Shut up, you dim mutt!"

Billy didn't, but it was a happy sort of barking, and when Poppy's mum opened the door, and hurried Poppy and Izzy in, he whisked around them, still barking, and wagging his tail frantically. It thumped against Izzy's legs, and she could see what Poppy meant about Billy being big – even his tail was strong!

He was a very strange-looking dog, Izzy thought, but in a nice way. He was mostly a golden-red colour, with white paws, white tummy, and a white blaze down the middle of his triangular nose. He stared up at Izzy with his head on one side, looking at her hopefully from small black eyes, as if she might have brought him something to eat.

"I think you need him over there," Izzy whispered, carefully patting Billy's head.

One of Poppy's brothers was disappearing up the stairs with a plate piled high with toast. "Hi, Mum." He waved at them vaguely.

"Just a light snack?" his mum called after him, sighing.

He didn't answer her, and Izzy realised he had earphones in.

"Right, well, there's obviously no point cooking dinner just yet. Your dad's not home anyway, Poppy, and Jake's at football till later. Why don't you two have a snack – biscuits, or you can have toast if that pig upstairs has left any bread. Then we can all have dinner when you get back from your walk."

At the word walk, Billy suddenly erupted into the kitchen and started barking again. He'd been sniffing Poppy's schoolbag in the hallway in case she'd brought anything slightly edible home.

"Mum! You have to spell that word out!" Poppy moaned. "Now he won't stop barking till we take him."

"Sorry!" Her mum quickly stuffed a handful of biscuits and a couple of apples into a plastic bag, and handed it to Izzy. "Take my phone with you, girls, just in case. Where are you going to go?" she half-shouted over the barking, which was getting louder as Poppy fetched Billy's lead off a hook in the under-stairs cupboard and he practically exploded with excitement.

"Umm, through the park and along the path by the river? That should wear him out a bit," Poppy suggested.

"OK. Back by half-five then?"

Poppy nodded, and the girls hurried out with Billy bouncing around them like an enormous puppy. Thankfully, he stopped barking once they got out of the front door, and he understood that they really were going for a walk – they hadn't just been teasing him with the lead. He set off at a fast pace, pulling hard on his collar, and making strangled noises.

"Is he OK?" Izzy asked worriedly. It sounded as though his collar was hurting him.

"He's fine, he's just a twit. Billy, heel!" Poppy said firmly, pulling him back.

Billy looked up at her mournfully. His long sloping nose made him quite good at looking mournful, Izzy thought. And despite Poppy saying he wasn't very clever, he definitely knew how to milk it.

"I'm not cross, you silly dog." Poppy patted him. "But you'll break your neck pulling like that."

"Couldn't you use some alternative therapies to calm him down a bit?" Izzy asked mischievously. She was expecting Poppy to tell her not to be so stupid, but instead her friend sighed.

"I did try. I borrowed Mum's Rescue Remedy, but it just made him sneeze. I think he ought to have a course of massage, actually, but Dad said there was no way he was paying for it."

Izzy snorted with laughter. She could just imagine Billy lying on a table with his legs in the air, being massaged. "You can't really do massage on dogs!" she said disbelievingly.

"Of course you can!" Poppy looked at her in surprise. "It's really good. Great for stress and relaxation. That's why Billy could do with it – he's just too mad all the time."

Izzy nodded. "I suppose it would calm him down,

if he'd keep still." She used to give her mum foot-rubs sometimes, she remembered, with a little jolt. Her mum had said it was blissful, and it made her want to fall asleep.

"There's a vet in Malton that does all sorts of alternative therapy for dogs. Massage. Acupuncture."

"Acupuncture? Like, with needles? They do that to dogs too?" Izzy sounded horrified.

"It's supposed to be really good for things like arthritis. Achy bones. Billy doesn't need that, though." Poppy eyed him. "Which is good, because to be honest, I can't see him letting anybody stick needles in him and keep them there. He howls if we even walk past the door of the vet's, and he hasn't had to go and have any vaccinations for ages."

"Really? He looks so – you know, big and brave."

"Nope. He's a wuss. But we love him anyway," Poppy told her happily as they headed into the park. "Just tell me if you see any other dogs coming up. I'm going to let his lead pull out."

"OK. Would he chase them?" Izzy looked round anxiously, but she couldn't see any other dogs at all.

"Probably not, but you never know. And because he's so big, if he gets in a scrap with another dog, their owner always seems to blame Billy, which is really

unfair. It's the little yappy dogs you need to watch, like Yorkshire Terriers, and Dachshunds – they can be really mean. And then their owner arrives, and yells at Billy for upsetting poor little Fluffball."

"I hadn't realised it was so exciting, having a dog," Izzy murmured, keeping a sharp eye out for Yorkshire Terriers.

Poppy grinned. "Billy's sort of a dog and a half. He always gets into everything. But he's great at home, too – he loves watching TV, he'll curl up with you for ages."

Izzy nodded. That sounded lovely – a big, cuddly dog to snuggle with when Dad was busy doing work stuff in the evenings.

"Look, if we go down that path there," Poppy pointed out through a gate, "we come to the river path. Have you been down there before?"

Izzy shook her head. "No. I've never been to this park, either, our house is the other side of town."

"It's a bit messy, but I like looking at the water, and Billy loves it. I think he smells water rats, or something like that. He goes sniffing along like a bloodhound."

Billy had caught the scent of the river path already, and he speeded up, his ears pricking with excitement.

"Wow…" Izzy looked around in surprise. The

river ran through the centre of town too, but it was all pretty there, with benches, and grassy banks. Lots of people went there for picnics.

"I know, it's such a mess." Poppy sighed. "What is it about shopping trolleys? I can see at least three of them."

The river bank was covered in litter, and the river itself looked like some weird piece of modern art, with stuff sticking out all over the place. As well as the shopping trolleys, there was a bike, and a bit of a boat, and Izzy was pretty sure she could see a mattress.

"Why do people dump all this stuff here?" she asked. "It would be really pretty, without all the rubbish."

There were benches, and a picnic table set further back on the grass, but she couldn't imagine anyone wanting to come and eat their lunch here. It was grim.

Poppy shrugged. "I guess once one person does it, everyone else thinks it's OK."

Billy was sniffing happily on the end of his long lead, poking his big nose in and out of the clumps of grass, and snapping at bees and butterflies.

"Don't eat that!" Poppy scolded, seeing him snap

his teeth shut millimetres away from a fat bumblebee. "It's not food! Remember last time? You were swollen up for days, dim dog."

Billy laid his ears back and looked ashamed of himself, but it only lasted a second before he was whiffling through the grasses again, his tail swishing back and forth in an excited blur.

"I don't see how you could get a boat down here." Izzy went closer to the water. "It's so full of stuff. You'd catch it all underneath."

"I don't think many narrowboats try and come down this bit," Poppy said. "This is like an extra little loop, you don't have to use it to get along the river towards the town centre." Then she jerked forward as Billy yanked on his lead. "Oi, Billy, stop it!"

But Billy was too excited to stop. He raced on, pulling Poppy after him.

"He's chasing something," Izzy said anxiously, trying to grab the lead and help Poppy pull, but the lead part was a thin cord, and it just ran through her fingers. "Ugh! It's a rat!"

"A water rat," Poppy panted grimly. "Billy! Stop! Ow!" She fell forwards, tripping over an old bag that someone had abandoned, and let go of the lead. "Oh no! Billy!"

RIVER RESCUE

The big golden dog shot off down the river path, his lead bouncing behind him, chasing something small and brown and furry.

Unfortunately, the small brown furry thing was a water rat – or at least it was a rat that could swim, because it jumped straight into the water, and Billy jumped after it.

Billy floundered about in the water, looking very surprised at himself – clearly he hadn't really meant to jump in, he'd just followed the rat. Luckily it didn't look to be too deep, and Billy seemed to have a natural doggy-paddle.

"You idiot dog!" Poppy muttered, crouching down by the bank. "Come here! Come on! He's going to be a nightmare to haul out, he's so heavy."

"Is there anything we can use to help?" Izzy looked around. "Something he could scramble on to?" There was so much junk, there had to be something.

"Oh no, Billy, stop, not that way!" Poppy wailed, and there was a hurt whimper from the water.

"What happened?" Izzy gasped. "Did something bite him?"

Poppy shook her head. "It's a bike – I didn't see it under the water, and I called him – now I think his paw's stuck in it."

Billy was whimpering and struggling, trying to pull his leg free, and getting panicky.

Izzy felt panicky too, and he wasn't even her dog, but Poppy lay down on the bank and stretched her arms out to him. "Shhh, shhh," she whispered, in a soothing whisper. "Keep still, baby, we'll get it out. Ow," she added, back in her normal voice.

"Tell me what to do," Izzy whispered, crouching next to her. "Can I lift the bike up, or anything?"

"Yes, lift that bit. And I'll pull Billy – if he's hurt he might not want anyone he doesn't know touching him. Pull! Now!"

Izzy yanked at the twisted bike wheel, and Poppy heaved on Billy's collar, and he half jumped, half fell out of the water, right on top of them both.

"Owwww," Izzy moaned. "He weighs a ton. Is he OK?"

Poppy wriggled. "Oooh, Billy, get off. Let's see your paw. Good boy. What a good dog."

Billy limped his way off them, and sat down, holding up his hurt paw, and looking miserable. "Poor baby," Poppy murmured, using that quiet whisper again. "It's not cut or anything. Perhaps he just banged it. Oh, Billy, you are a monster," she said, giving him a big hug. "I'm really sorry, Izzy. I wish this hadn't happened when you were with us."

"I don't! If you'd been on your own, you might not have been able to get him out," Izzy said worriedly.

"No more loose lead along here," Poppy sighed. "It wouldn't have been so dangerous if it weren't for those stupid people who dumped the bike."

Billy put his paw to the ground, and stared at it anxiously, as though he wasn't sure it was still working, but when he tried to walk he was hardly limping at all.

"He looks OK," said Izzy hopefully. "Just wet. And a bit muddy."

"Yeah, I think he was lucky." Poppy shivered. "Let's get home." She looked Izzy up and down, and then glanced at her own school uniform. "I think he wiped the mud off on us. You look *awful*!"

"So do you!" Izzy sighed, holding out the skirt of her summer dress   all muddy and torn.

"I can lend you something." Poppy gave her a hug. "Don't worry. I'll explain to your dad."

"What happened?" Poppy's mum shrieked, as they let themselves in. They'd been hoping to sneak upstairs quietly, and say that Izzy just fancied getting out of her uniform, but unfortunately Poppy's mum had been coming down the stairs as they came in.

"Billy fell in the river," Poppy admitted.

"He was chasing a rat – it wasn't Poppy's fault," Izzy added quickly.

"Are you all right?" Poppy's mum shot down the stairs. "Did you fall in too? Are you hurt?"

"Just wet. Billy splashed all over us," Poppy explained.

"That dog!" Poppy's mum glared at him.

"He got stuck in an old bike someone had thrown in," Izzy told her, hoping to make her less cross with him.

"Oh dear, it's such a mess down there. You'll have to stop walking him by the river, Poppy. Ugh, look at him, he's covered in mud."

"Shall we put him in the bath?" Poppy suggested. "And please don't say we can't go down there, Mum, it's his favourite walk."

"It could have been his last walk, if you couldn't get him out," her mum snapped. "Yes, you'd better bath him. And then you two can have showers. I'll go and make you some hot chocolate. Do you like chocolate, Izzy?"

"Please." Izzy nodded. Even though it was June, she still felt cold and muddy and horrible. Hot chocolate and a shower sounded excellent.

"OK. Once we get close to the bathroom, I'll pull, you push," Poppy instructed, running up the stairs and leaving Izzy staring after her. "Billy! Come on, boy!"

Billy bounded up the stairs – his paw had had a miraculous recovery on the way home. He'd been able to bark himself silly at a fat black cat, and it seemed to have cheered him up no end.

"Shut the door!" Poppy shrieked, as Izzy hurried after her. "He's going to notice where he is in a minute, shut the door!"

Izzy slammed the bathroom door shut just as Billy clocked the bath, and tried to exit his collar backwards. He stood in the corner of the bathroom, staring reproachfully at Poppy and Izzy.

"Your fault for going ratting in a river," Poppy said sternly. "We have to get the mud off you, or Mum'll have you living in the garden. It's *Top Gear* tonight, Billy, you want to be allowed on the sofa."

"He likes *Top Gear*?" Izzy laughed.

"Yup. His favourite programme. He even knows the music, he rushes in when he hears it's on."

"How are we going to get him in the bath?" Izzy asked doubtfully, as Poppy began to run the water.

"And what's that you're putting in the water?"

Poppy was adding drips of something from a little bottle. "Lavender oil. To calm him down a bit. And it smells nice," she added sensibly. "He stinks of river. You can't put bubble bath in, it isn't good for dogs' skin. We could probably use Mum's expensive organic stuff, but she'd recognise the smell on him, and then she'd kill me. And we get him in by picking him up and putting him in, of course."

Izzy looked at Billy, backed stubbornly into the corner of the bathroom. Then she looked at herself and Poppy. Billy was huge. And heavy. "Umm…"

"He isn't really that heavy," Poppy assured her.

"But will he let us pick him up?"

"He'll wriggle like mad, but we can do it. Then once he's in, one of us just has to hold on to his collar, and he'll stay still while we wash the mud off. OK. That should be enough. He doesn't like too much water round his legs." She giggled. "So who knows why he decided to jump into a river. Stupid dog."

Billy saw Poppy approaching, with a meaningful look in her eyes, and moaned. Izzy had never realised dogs could moan, but that was definitely what it was.

"You're filthy," Poppy told him sternly. "We have to get the mud off. Right, Izzy, I've got the front, you've got the back – that's the lighter end," she added encouragingly.

Izzy thought it was more important that it was the end without the teeth, but she didn't say so. Even though Bull Terriers had a fierce reputation, Billy seemed quite friendly and gentle. But that was before they'd tried to heave him into a bath.

The bathroom door opened suddenly, and Poppy shrieked as Billy attempted to make a quick getaway.

"Alex, stop him!"

Billy was attempting to shoot between the legs of one of Poppy's twin older brothers. But Alex squashed his knees together, so he was almost riding Billy, and grabbed his collar.

Izzy laughed. "You look like you're in a rodeo," she said shyly, as Alex stared at her.

He snorted. "Oh. Yeah, Billy would make a good bucking bronco. Aww, Poppy, he's covered in mud, it's all over my trousers now."

"Durr," Poppy said unsympathetically. "That's why we're trying to bath him, idiot."

"You two'll never get him in there," Alex said. And he grabbed Billy round the chest, groaning with the effort, and dumped him in the bath so quickly that Billy didn't have time to realise what was going on.

Even though there was hardly any water, a tidal wave still splashed over the edge of the bath.

Billy's claws scrabbled frantically, and he howled, and tried to jump out, but Alex had hold of his collar. "Hurry up then! Wash him! I'm getting soaked here," he growled to Poppy.

"Thanks, Alex!" Poppy started rubbing the mud off Billy's legs, and Izzy tried to swoosh water over his back, while Billy moaned miserably. The smell of wet dog rapidly overpowered the lavender oil.

"I think he's clean," Poppy said at last. "Or at least the water's so dirty there's no point washing him any more."

"Do we have to lift him out now?" Izzy asked, looking anxiously at Alex. He was going to get even wetter, heaving a soaking wet dog out of the bath.

Alex laughed. "Nope." He let go off Billy's collar, and stood back, pulling Izzy with him.

Billy took about two seconds to realise he no longer had to be in the bath, and launched himself out with an expression of great joy on his face. Water slopped everywhere, and as soon as he hit the bath mat, he shook himself madly, spraying more all over the place.

"Now you see why there was no point changing

first," Poppy pointed out, holding her arm across her face. "Have you stopped yet, Billy?" She smothered him in an old towel that she'd pulled out of the bottom of the airing cupboard. "Mum keeps the worst towels just for him."

They rubbed him dry all over and eventually a spotless and offended-looking dog burst out of the bathroom, and hurtled down the stairs.

"He's going to hide in his basket," Poppy explained. "Look, I've rinsed the mud out of the bath now, you have a quick shower. I'll just go and find you some stuff to borrow."

"Thanks." Izzy eyed her school dress and cardigan – they were even wetter now.

Ten minutes or so later, she headed downstairs, still damp, but much warmer, and wearing Poppy's jeans and a cute purple T-shirt.

Poppy's mum pushed a mug of hot chocolate towards her.

"Thanks. Poppy is just having her shower. Alex might want some chocolate too, Billy got him really wet."

Billy heard his name, and glared suspiciously over the edge of his basket.

The door opened, and another teenage boy

clumped into the kitchen. Poppy's mum sighed. "Between you lot and the dog, I'm going to be spending the weekend cleaning mud out of this house. It's all very well taking your boots off, but look at your socks, Jake!"

"Sorry, the field was a bit muddy," he admitted.

Izzy stared at him over her mug. If Poppy's mum hadn't called him Jake, she would have been sure he was Alex, somehow muddied up. They looked exactly the same.

"This is Poppy's friend, Izzy," Poppy's mum added. "Billy jumped in the river, you'll have to queue for a shower after your sister."

"Is he OK?" Jake peered at Billy, who was huddled up in his basket, as if he didn't want anyone to notice him.

"I think he's sulking because he had to have a bath," Izzy said, feeling quite amazed at herself. She hardly ever spoke to people she didn't know. But there was something about this mad, muddy house that made her feel less shy than usual.

Jake nodded. "He would be. He hates baths. See you later, Izzy."

"Usually, he'd take off all his football stuff and just stuff it in the machine," Poppy's mum whispered to

Izzy as Jake went upstairs. "He's being polite because you're here."

Izzy giggled, and tried not to spit chocolate everywhere.

"Shall we go and watch a film?" Poppy arrived, and grabbed her chocolate. "Thanks, Mum."

"You won't have time for a film, dinner won't be long," her mum pointed out.

"Mmm, washing Billy took ages. OK. We'll just put the TV on."

They curled up on the sofa happily, and Izzy thought how nice it was not to feel guilty about watching a stupid girly soap. Sometimes it was what she felt like, but she knew Dad hated them, so she hardly ever put them on.

They were just happily criticising one of the girls' hairstyles when Poppy frowned, then turned to Izzy with her finger to her lips. "Listen!" she whispered, turning the sound on the TV down a little.

"What is it?" Izzy whispered back, a little anxiously.

"Alex! On the phone, ssshhh!" Poppy tiptoed closer to the garden door.

Alex was sitting outside on a bench – he obviously didn't realise that the door was open, and the girls could hear him.

Izzy felt a bit guilty eavesdropping, but Poppy clearly didn't. Perhaps it was a brother/sister thing that you just didn't understand if you were an only one? Poppy's eyes were glittering with gleeful excitement.

"He is! He's talking to a girl!" she hissed to Izzy. "And I'm practically certain it's not Lucy. She lives up the road, he's been seeing her on-again off-again for ages."

Alex was talking very quietly so the girls found themselves leaning dangerously round the door to hear. But he was so intent on his conversation that he didn't notice them at all.

"OK. Yeah. Tomorrow night, then. Bye, Maddy."

He finished the call and jumped up so quickly that he caught Poppy by surprise, and she fell backwards into the doorway giggling, and half squashing Izzy.

"Oi! Poppy, were you listening?" Alex stopped staring happily down at his phone and advanced on Poppy, looking menacing.

"Of course I was!" Poppy kept laughing. "Who's *Maddy*, Alex?"

"No one!" he snapped.

"OK, I'll just ask Jake."

"Don't you dare!"

"Hang on. Maddy…" Poppy stared at him, her eyes widening. "It's not that girl from your canoe club that he's fancied for ages?"

Alex went red. "He never even spoke to her," he muttered. "I gave him loads of time. We just got talking…"

"He'll kill you!" Poppy stood up, folding her arms, and shook her head sadly. "You are *dead*."

"She doesn't belong to him," Alex muttered, but he looked guilty. "Don't tell him, Poppy."

"Why not? He's going to find out anyway."

"Yeah, well, I want him to find out gradually. If I get together with Maddy, I'll tell him then, OK?"

"You really owe me, if I don't tell him," Poppy pointed out.

"I helped you bath the dog!"

"This is worth way more than bathing the dog!" Poppy squeaked. "And I'm holding you to it. Just wait."

Alex stomped out of the living room, muttering, and Poppy hugged Izzy.

"Oh, that was so funny. Now we just have to wait till we need a big, big favour…"

FOUR

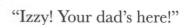

"Izzy! Your dad's here!"

Izzy and Poppy were upstairs in Poppy's room, listening to some music after they'd had dinner, and plotting ways to call in the favour Alex owed them.

Izzy picked up her damp, muddy school dress and cardigan, and shook them out – she'd been trying not to think about them, and she'd almost forgotten.

"Is your dad going to be annoyed?" Poppy asked apologetically. "I'll tell him it was my fault. And Billy's."

"I shouldn't think he'll mind that much," Izzy said hopefully. But it was quite a new dress, and she'd torn it on the sharp mudguard of the bike. Dad wouldn't shout at her or anything, but he would sigh, in that tired sort of way.

They galloped down the stairs, and found Izzy's dad making a fuss over Billy. He was scratching the big dog behind the ears, and Billy was leaning against his legs with a blissed-out look on his face.

"Wow, he likes you!" Poppy said in surprise. Billy looked so relaxed he was about to fall over.

"My dad used to have one of these – Grandad Pete, Izzy. His was called Patch, he looked like a pirate. That was when I was your age, though." Her dad hugged her. "Oh, you got changed!" he said, sounding surprised.

"We got a bit wet –"

"Billy was chasing –"

"The girls had an accident –"

Izzy, Poppy and her mum all tried to explain at once.

"An accident? Are you OK?" Izzy's dad looked worriedly down at Billy, as though he thought the Bull Terrier might have hurt Izzy.

"We're fine, Dad. But Billy chased a rat into the river, down by the park, and then he got stuck in an old bike that someone had thrown in! We had to rescue him, and I tore my school dress. A little bit." Izzy held it up apologetically.

Her dad frowned at the tear. "I reckon I can probably mend that. You didn't get hurt? And Billy didn't?"

Poppy shook her head. "He was lucky, though. He sort of caught his paw in the bike wheel, but we managed to pull it out without hurting him."

"There's so much junk in the water down there," Izzy explained. "Three shopping trolleys, Dad! And there was a TV."

"And a fridge on the bank," Poppy added.

"Is that the bit of the river that runs through Illroy Park?" Izzy's dad asked. "With a footpath along it?"

"Yes, but the footpath's where loads of the rubbish is," Poppy explained.

"I've told Poppy she's going to have to stop taking Billy down there," her mum said apologetically. "I'm really sorry – I shouldn't have let the girls go."

"No, don't worry about that, you couldn't have known Billy would go diving in."

Poppy's mum sighed. "You don't know Billy. I should have guessed!"

Izzy's dad grinned, and scratched Billy's ears again. Billy groaned happily, and slumped further to the floor.

"It's a real pity that it's in such a mess, though. I haven't been there for years, but it used to be a great place for walks – your grandad and I used to take Patch down there, actually, Izzy. It's such a shame.

Anyway, we'd better get going. What do you say to Poppy's mum, Izzy?"

Izzy rolled her eyes. She wasn't six. "Thanks for having me," she said. "And see you on Monday, Poppy."

"So, did you have a good time?" Izzy's dad asked her as they were driving home. He was looking at her worriedly, she could tell.

"Watch the road, Dad!"

"Sorry, sorry. I was thinking about you – while I had my tea all on my own."

"Oh, Dad!" Izzy gazed at him guiltily.

"I don't mean it! I just wanted to know that you were all right. You were, weren't you?"

"I had a fab time," Izzy promised him. "I'm really sorry about the dress, though. It was one of the newish ones, too."

"Well, like I said, I think I can mend it. Or if I can't, I'm sure your gran could."

"Was the river really a nice place to go, before?"

Her dad nodded. "Beautiful. Still a bit wild, but that was good. I saw a kingfisher down there once. And there were some rare plants, I'm sure. I'm really surprised it's been left to get into such a state." He glanced down at Izzy. "How about we go down there

on our bikes tomorrow? Ride through the park and along the river?"

"You don't have to work tomorrow?" Izzy asked delightedly.

"Nope, got my invoices done while you were at Poppy's tonight. I fancy a bike ride. And maybe a picnic."

"Whoa." Izzy's dad stopped in the middle of the pathway, and stared around. "I didn't realise it would be this bad."

Izzy braked, and slid up beside him. "I know, it's a mess, isn't it?"

"It looks like a junk yard." Her dad sighed, staring around at the rubbish scattered all over the path, and in the water. "It used to be so beautiful here, Iz. It's probably hard to believe, but it really did…" He got off his bike, and leaned it up against one of the benches, and went wandering through the mess, kicking at things here and there. "Who dumps a whole load of old newspapers by the side of a river? Why not just put them in the recycling? I don't understand some people." He stopped, looking down at an old piece of wood. "I thought so. Look at this, Iz." He swept the grass away from the board with one hand,

and Izzy came to see over his shoulder.

"Illroy Riverside Nature Reserve," she read out. "Please keep dogs on the lead." She laughed sadly. "We did, but it didn't help much. That's really sad. What can have happened to let it get like this?"

"I should think people just forgot about it, and it was too expensive to keep it properly looked after." Her dad shook his head.

"Could your Rescue group help sort it out, Dad?" Izzy asked suddenly.

Her dad looked round with a sigh. "I'd really like to suggest it to them, but we're a bit short of money right now. Buying all those trees for that little green patch behind the old people's home cost us a lot. We'd need to do some fundraising first to get this all sorted, and we've already promised to do some clean-up over in the woods close to your school too."

Izzy nodded. Her dad had been asked to join a local environmental group a few months before. It was organised by somebody he'd done some garden landscaping for. They planted trees and bulbs around the area, and every so often organised a big Rescue Weekend, where they hired a skip and cleared up litter and junk. This neglected bit of river sounded just right for them.

"I'll definitely mention it at our next meeting, though," her dad agreed. "It's just the sort of thing we'd want to do. Actually, I'm surprised no one's mentioned it already. I suppose it's a bit out of the way."

"I should think people only come here when they want to dump rubbish," Izzy agreed sadly. "I don't think I want to eat the picnic here, Dad."

"No, definitely not. We'll go further on, round to the main bit of the river – it's a lot nicer to look at there."

They got back on their bikes and, ten minutes later, they were sitting on the grass, watching two swans gliding along with their beaks in the air, looking extremely grand.

"I bet they wouldn't go down that bit of river," Izzy said, between bites of ham sandwich.

"Certainly not. Not nearly clean enough for those posh swans."

Izzy chewed thoughtfully as she watched the swans disappearing round the curve of the water. If it was only money that was stopping Dad's Rescue group cleaning up the river, maybe there was something she and Poppy and Emily and Maya could do to help? Could they raise some money somehow? Mr Finlay had said they needed a new project. It would be nice to do something that was really close to home, too.

She bit into an apple, smiling to herself. A new project. Something they could really help with. It sounded excellent!

On Monday she hurried to find Poppy in the playground, and smiled to herself at the difference from Friday morning.

Emily and Maya were already there, as the school bus had been on time for once, and they waved to her.

"Was your dad really OK about your dress?" Poppy asked anxiously. "I told Emily and Maya what happened," she added.

"That dog!" Emily shook her head. "He's a menace."

"He's a very nice menace," Izzy said, smiling.

"He's still sulking about us giving him a bath," Poppy sighed. "He's hardly talking to me."

Emily snickered, and Poppy elbowed her. "You know what I mean."

"My dad didn't mind that much, and we went to see my gran yesterday, she's going to mend it for me. I showed my dad the river too – we went for a bike

ride down there on Saturday. He was really upset at how messy it was."

"It is pretty bad," Poppy agreed.

"He says it used to be beautiful, and we found a board that said it was a nature reserve."

Poppy looked disbelieving. "Really? I've never seen rare birds flying in and out of the old fridge, Izzy."

"Well, I shouldn't think it's much use as one now – not with all that rubbish messing up the water and everything. But it used to be. And I bet it could be again, if it was cleaned up." She looked at the others hopefully. "Dad belongs to a clean-up group, they take on projects just like that. But they've spent all their money on trees."

"Are you thinking we could help? Like Mr Finlay said?" Maya asked excitedly.

"It would be a really cool project," Izzy said. She was so glad Maya liked the idea – she was the one who'd first thought of the fashion show, and Izzy couldn't help feeling that she had to approve this before it could happen. It was Maya who'd started them off working as a team.

But Emily was scowling. "It doesn't sound cool at all! Picking up litter on a messy river bank? It sounds dead boring."

"I know it's not as exciting as organising a fashion show—" Izzy started to say, but Emily interrupted.

"Of course it isn't!" Emily stared at her disgustedly.

Izzy sighed, and tried to tell herself it was just the way Emily was. Stroppy. Izzy had a feeling it was to do with having two very annoying, very loud younger brothers (and a baby sister who, although she didn't get on Emily's nerves as much, meant that Emily's mum was always busy).

Emily had a habit of making snap decisions and then sticking to them like glue, even when really she knew she was wrong. Izzy liked her most of the time, but sometimes she could be a real pain. Izzy sighed, and tried not to get upset. "I'm not saying we ought to go and clean up the river – though I'd like to join in, I think it *would* be cool, actually. If you listen, I think we ought to help raise some money, so my dad's Rescue group can do the tidying up."

"What do they need the money for?" Maya asked. "Isn't it just picking up some rubbish?"

"They'd have to hire a skip – and maybe some other equipment. You haven't seen it, Maya, it isn't just litter. There was half an old boat, and the bike that Billy got stuck in."

"And the mattress in the water, that would be really

hard to get out," Poppy agreed. "They might need one of those little diggers, with a grab on. Something like that. I bet they cost a lot to hire."

"Exactly." Izzy sighed. "Maybe we couldn't…"

"I bet we could!" Maya was looking interested. "I'm not sure how, yet… Who does that bit of river belong to?"

Izzy shook her head. "I don't know. The sign said it was a nature reserve. The council? My dad could find out, or someone else from the Rescue group."

"We ought to do that first." Maya nodded. "Otherwise we might raise all the money and get down there with a skip, only for someone to come and tell us to get lost."

"We?" Emily muttered. "Us?"

"It would be fun!" Poppy put an arm round her. "You wouldn't want to raise money for something and then not go and help. It would be a real shame. And if we could clean it up, it would feel so good afterwards, Ems! We could go there and know that we'd helped make it nice again."

"Oh, all right…" Emily growled. "I suppose. It just sounds boring. And muddy."

Izzy giggled. "You should have seen us on Friday."

Poppy nodded. "Yeah, waterproofs all round if we do go and help. But we need to work out how to raise some money first."

Maya was frowning. "Do you think other people from school would want to come and join in? If your dad's group worked out when they might do their clean-up session, we could put posters up, try and get more people to come and help."

"I think they'd probably choose a weekend – that's what they usually do for a big project. I reckon all that rubbish would take at least a weekend to clear."

"How much money do you think we'd need to raise?" Poppy asked, and Izzy shrugged.

"I honestly don't know. I'll ask Dad what he thinks after school," she promised.

But when she dashed out of school to find him that afternoon, with Poppy and the others chasing after her, her dad was on his mobile, frowning gloomily. He waved when he saw her coming, but then he went back to his conversation, and sighed. "No, absolutely. Well, it was just a thought. We can't do everything. OK. Talk soon." He ended the call, and looked down at Izzy. "Hey, sweetheart. Hi, Poppy."

"This is Maya, and this is Emily, Dad, you remember?"

Her dad smiled and nodded. "Course."

"Dad, I was telling them about the river. Do you think if we raised some money for the skip and stuff, the Rescue group would do a clean-up weekend there?"

Her dad looked at her in surprise. "Great minds think alike, Iz. I was just talking to Richard – the one who organises the group."

Izzy beamed, but then she realised that her dad was looking disappointed, and his phone call hadn't exactly sounded enthusiastic either. "Oh no! He didn't think it was a good idea?" she asked sadly.

Her dad shook his head. "He thought it was a great idea! But the group have already got the next two Rescue Weekends planned, and then they stop for the summer holidays. He says he'd love the group to help but he just can't ask people to commit to another weekend. They're all volunteers, you see."

Izzy nodded. "I suppose so."

Emily let out an enormous sigh. "I knew it was going to end up being us doing it," she moaned.

Izzy looked round at her. "What, you mean you

think we should just do it ourselves?"

Emily shrugged. "Why not? But I'm warning you now, Izzy, I'm going to complain the whole weekend. And I'd better not get wet."

FIVE

Izzy's dad laughed. "Well, I'm up for it too."

"Really?" Izzy said happily. "Even without all the people from Rescue?"

Her dad nodded. "Why not? If we ask around, I'm sure we can find a few people for a one-off."

"Oooh! We could get the local paper to put in something asking for people to help! I've still got the email address the journalist gave us." Maya giggled. "I think he's a bit scared of my mum, I bet they'll put a bit in about it."

"What are you girls plotting?" Poppy's mum asked, seeing them all hovering round Izzy and her dad.

"We're going to clean up the river!" Poppy told her excitedly.

Her mum frowned. "What, the bit where Billy went in the water? I'm not sure that's a very good idea, Poppy."

"Why not?" Poppy stared at her in surprise, and the other girls looked worried.

"Well, from what you said, Poppy, it's dangerous! Billy nearly cut his paws – who knows what other stuff you girls might hurt yourselves on."

Izzy's dad nodded. "I hadn't thought of that – I wasn't going to let them go down there on their own, though. I'd definitely be with them, and the girls are thinking of getting lots of people to join in. Sort of a public appeal."

Poppy's mum sighed. "It would be nice to get it cleaned up, then Billy wouldn't miss out on his favourite walk."

"You could come and help too, Mum!" Poppy pointed out.

Her mum nodded reluctantly. "I can't say it would be my favourite way to spend a weekend, but I can't just dump you on Izzy's dad and go home, can I?"

"Dad could come too," Poppy suggested.

"Hmm. You might have to work on him. Emily, aren't you and Maya supposed to be on the bus?"

"Eeek! See you tomorrow!" Emily yelped. "I'll ask my dad if he'll help too."

Maya waved. "Don't forget about the council, Izzy," she called, as they raced off.

"What was that about the council?" Izzy's dad asked, as they walked to his truck.

"Maya said we ought to find out who the river bank belongs to, and make sure we're allowed to go and tidy it up." Izzy frowned. "I think they ought to be grateful, but I suppose she's right. You don't know who it belongs to, do you?"

Her dad shook his head. "No, I'd assumed it was the council, though. But maybe not – they'd probably have sorted it out if it was theirs."

"Who do we ask?" Izzy wondered.

"We'll ring up the environment department, see what they say."

Izzy was so anxious to get her plan going that she refused the offer of a snack – chocolate biscuits! – and hurried her dad to the phone. She'd even found him the number, but he had a mouthful of biscuit, and just made faces at her.

"Fine! I'll do it." She didn't really like calling people she didn't know, but her dad was just being too annoying.

Her dad watched in surprise as she made the phone call, scribbling notes on a bit of paper.

"What did they say?" he asked eagerly, as she put the phone down.

"It does belong to the council, and we have to write to them to get permission to tidy it up!" Izzy scowled. "She said it was because the council could get into trouble if someone was hurt. She gave me an email address for the person to ask though, so it might be a bit quicker than a letter. And they'll lend us litter pickers, and high-vis vests to wear, and gloves. But they can't provide a skip, we'll have to hire one, or just take everything to the tip."

"We could use my van for that, or some of it, anyway. We'll probably need a skip as well." Her dad was watching her, and smiling.

"What?" Izzy stared back, wondering if she had something on her face. "Why are you looking at me like that?"

"I can't believe you just rang up the council!" He shook his head. "What happened to my shy little mouse daughter? And where did you come from?"

Izzy shrugged, but she'd gone pink. It was true. A few weeks ago, she'd never have dared. "I just really want it to happen," she said. "And I need to make a list."

"Not another one!" Her dad grinned.

"Funny, Dad. And I have to go online. She said there's a leaflet you can download about clean-ups from the council website. I need to do the email too. How much does a skip cost, Dad?"

"Depends on the size – a good big one is about a hundred and fifty pounds."

"Wow," Izzy muttered. "That's a lot. But I can't think of anything else we need to buy, except paper for making posters."

"Oh, and bin bags as well. That leaflet might tell you some more stuff," her dad suggested.

"I wish we knew if the council people were going to say yes." Izzy sighed. "I suppose we could start planning fundraising ideas anyway."

"I can't believe it takes so much fuss to organise tidying something up," Emily moaned at break. They hadn't had time to talk it over properly before school. "It ought to be the council's job to tidy it up anyway! Why aren't they just saying sorry, we've been useless and it's got in a mess? They should be *paying* us!"

Izzy nodded. For once, she totally agreed with Emily. They should get someone to take a photo in case it never happened again.

"They ought to say yes, though," Maya said thoughtfully. "I mean, why would they say no? So if we are allowed, when shall we do it?"

"I thought maybe three weekends from now?" Izzy suggested. "That gives us time to put posters up, and send the information to the paper. But the tricky thing is that we need to raise the money for a skip, and some bin bags. My dad said a skip could be as much as a hundred and fifty pounds."

Maya nodded. "How are we going to get all that?" she murmured.

"Food," Poppy said firmly. "Don't you remember the cake sale we had for the Guide Dogs last term?" It had been their class charity. "We made fifty pounds then, and I bet we could have charged more for those cakes. People pay loads!"

"Yes, and we ought to have it on a Tuesday," Emily agreed. "On a Tuesday, at lunchtime. Tuesday lunch is always awful, it's random-pasta-and-stew-day. We'll sell out in minutes."

Poppy laughed. "Good idea. And that means we could make the cakes at the weekend. My mum won't mind helping make some..." She trailed off. "But not enough for a whole cake sale. That would take a whole lot of butter and sugar and stuff."

"No, we'll have to do what we did for the refreshments at the show, buy the ingredients, and pay ourselves back from what we make," Izzy agreed.

"We could all make some, couldn't we?"

Emily nodded. "I'll have to make something Toby and James don't like, otherwise they'll never get as far as school. Minty cakes. Neither of them can stand mint. Can you get mint cake?" she added doubtfully.

"Peppermint creams?" Poppy suggested. "They're easy. And most people like them, even if Toby and James wouldn't."

"Oooh, yes! I love them. And I can make them peppermint fish, because we're raising money to clean up the river." Emily beamed.

"Let's go and ask Mrs Angel if we can do it," Maya suggested, jumping up from the bench.

"What, now?" Izzy asked, rather uncertainly. Mrs Angel was not the easiest person to chat to.

Maya shrugged. "We could at least ask Mrs Brooker if we could talk to her." Mrs Brooker was the school secretary, and she acted like she was Mrs Angel's bodyguard sometimes.

"Oh! Look!" Emily twisted Maya round. "Mrs Angel, talking to Mr Finlay."

Poppy grabbed Izzy's arm, and pulled her across the playground to the main door where the two teachers were standing. "Excellent. Mr Finlay told us to find a new project, he'll have to help us with Mrs Angel."

Mr Finlay looked slightly daunted when the four of them arrived in front of him, smiling hopefully. "Did you want something, girls?"

"We've thought of a new project," Izzy told him. "You did say we should," she added, when he looked lost. "There's a really messy bit of river bank at the bottom of Illroy Park – it used to be a nature reserve, and we think it still is, officially. It should be really beautiful, and my dad says there used to be rare birds, and plants." She took a deep breath, and watched Mrs Angel. "We've applied to the council for permission to organise a clean-up weekend and sort it out, in a few weeks' time. But we need to raise some money first, to hire a skip. So please can we have a cake sale?"

Emily nudged her.

"Er, on a Tuesday? Next Tuesday?" Izzy added. "And would it be all right to mention the clean-up in the school newsletter for the next couple of Fridays? And put posters up?"

Mrs Angel shook her head. "You four girls amaze me. I would have thought the fashion show would be enough for a while."

"Izzy's got the organising bug," Poppy told the head. "She's very good at it."

"A future head teacher in the making." Mrs Angel smiled at her, and Izzy tried not to look horrified. She couldn't imagine anything worse than being a teacher. Imagine having to try to tell people like Ali and Lucy and Elspeth to shut up and get on with their work. She would have a nervous breakdown after a week.

"A community clean-up sounds like a very good idea, girls. You may certainly hold a cake sale. Mr Finlay will help you, I'm sure." She smiled at him, and hurried away, leaving him staring after her indignantly.

The girls beamed at him, and Mr Finlay sighed. "All right. What needs doing?"

"Nothing, sir," Izzy promised. "Unless you feel like making some cakes?"

Izzy had enough pocket money saved up to buy quite a lot of cake ingredients, so that weekend she turned the kitchen into a cake production line. She had decided to make chocolate fairy cakes and cornflake cakes – she was sure they were the things that sold best, as almost everyone loved chocolate. Though

Emily was right – on a Tuesday lunch time, even the grottiest-looking cake would probably sell. She mixed up a big batch of green icing while the fairy cakes were cooking, and then cut out lots of tiny little orange icing fish. She knew goldfish wouldn't really be swimming in the river (probably there weren't any fish at all there right now) but orange looked better than grey or brown.

On Monday night she made chocolate chip cookies as well, and when they set off for school on Tuesday morning, every available surface of the truck was covered in plates of cakes wrapped in clingfilm – her dad even had one on his lap.

"Oh, Izzy, you've made loads!" Maya said admiringly, waiting by the gate to help her carry them in.

"Has anyone else brought any?" Izzy asked hopefully. They'd told all their class about the fundraising, and asked for more cakes if people could bring them.

Maya rolled her eyes. "Quite a few – and guess what! Ali made some!"

"Really?" Izzy stared at her. "Ali made cakes for us?"

"Yup."

"Well, make sure you tell me which ones they are because I was going to buy some to take home, and I don't want to die poisoned." Izzy shook her head. "Do you think she's still trying to get you to be friends with her then?"

Maya nodded. "She keeps smiling at me. And she asked me to be her partner for tennis in PE yesterday, did you see?"

Izzy shook her head. "I was probably thinking about cake recipes," she admitted. "She's not giving up, is she?"

"Not sure she knows the meaning of it," Maya muttered.

Mrs Angel had said they could put all the cakes in the hall, on a couple of tables – they would have to move them out to the playground at lunch time, when the hall got turned into a lunch room. Mrs Angel said it wasn't fair to put cakes right next to the school lunches – they had to be a little distance away…

Poppy and Emily were already there, admiring the cakes, and Izzy stared delightedly at the full tables. "There's loads! Oh, Emily, you made your peppermint fish! They look fab!"

Emily smiled proudly at the plates of fish – they

were quite big, with silver balls for eyes, and loopy dribbles of chocolate to make scales. "Good, aren't they? I got Mum to help me find a recipe, and she was having so much fun she made Dad take the boys out for a bike ride last night, and me and Mum and Sukie made them. Well, we gave Sukie some mixture and she made worms out of it. There are fifty of them," she added proudly. "And Mum says we can donate the ingredients. She bought them for me, and I was going to pay her back, but she said it was a good cause, and we had a great time doing them, so she doesn't mind."

"That's brilliant," Izzy said happily. "And guess what, my dad has a friend who works for a skip company, and he rang him and asked how much a skip would be, and they're giving us a discount! But we have to try and get in the paper, and say thank you to them for giving us it cheap. Sampson Skip Hire, they're called. And if he's not driving skips around, my dad's friend's going to come and help too!"

"So how much do you reckon we need to raise?" Maya asked anxiously.

"The skip's only going to be fifty pounds. So we need to cover some of the costs of the cakes, and have enough for some bin bags too."

"I looked at bin bags in the supermarket when we went to buy the cake ingredients," Poppy put in. "How many will we need? Maybe a hundred? That would be about fifteen pounds."

"One cake sale isn't going to get us more than sixty-five pounds," Izzy sighed.

"I don't know, there's an awful lot of cake," Emily pointed out, waving at the full tables.

"Who made that gorgeous big one with all the sweets on top?" Izzy asked, noticing a huge purple iced cake, covered in jelly jewels, which was hidden at the back of one of the tables.

"Anna did, and I helped with the icing and the sweets." Maya grinned. "Anna loves making cakes but with Mum and Dad away so much, she doesn't make them very often. I think she'd love us to have a cake sale every week." Anna was Maya's mum's housekeeper, and she looked after Maya whenever her parents were away. Maya eyed the cake hungrily. "Even though it's making me starving, it does seem a pity to slice it up. But no one from school's going to buy a whole cake."

"Guess the weight of the cake!" Poppy yelled suddenly. "They had that at the fete we went to last weekend! We make people pay fifty pence to guess.

That's bound to raise more money than cutting it up."

"And the person who gets it right gets the cake?" Izzy nodded. "That sounds brilliant."

"Oh, except we don't know how much it weighs…" Poppy sighed.

"Mrs Brooker's got some scales in the office, for weighing parcels before she sends them in the post. I've seen her do it." Izzy looked at the cake, and shook her head. "I'm not carrying it, I'd die if I dropped it. You do it, Maya."

They hurried Maya down the corridors to the office, with Emily marching in front, calling, "Gangway!" and "Cake coming through!"

"This is good, lots of people are admiring it," Poppy pointed out. The bell had just gone, and school was heaving. "You have to guess the weight of it," she told some Year Four girls who were staring hungrily at the jelly jewels. "We'll bring it round all the classes later. Hopefully," she added.

Mrs Brooker only sighed when they arrived at her office begging for scales. She handed them over, and some paper to make lists of weights. "I'm not looking, girls. But I want a go. I'm guessing, mmm, one kilogram, six hundred and thirty-four grams."

She handed Izzy fifty pence.

"No, it isn't nearly that much, surely." One of the mums who'd come in to order a new uniform peered at the cake.

"Would you like a guess?" Izzy asked hopefully.

"Go on then. But if I win, you're not to give it to Max! It'll never come home. One kilo exactly. That's easy to remember."

"A pound already and we haven't even started the cake sale," Izzy said smugly, jingling the box she'd brought for the money as they hurried to their classroom.

By twenty minutes into lunch time, Izzy was wishing she'd brought a bigger box. She was scrabbling around trying to find change, and write down people's names on the Guess the Weight of the Cake list at the same time.

"Why are my cakes shoved at the back?" Ali snapped at her, and Izzy's heart thumped painfully as she tried to think of something to say.

"They aren't..." she muttered feebly. But they were. Mostly because they didn't look all that good. Izzy thought that Ali had done what she usually ended up doing – not waited for them to cool down before she put the icing on, so it just ran off the top and left bald icingless cake in the middle.

"If you don't want them, I'll have them back!" Ali snarled, but Maya turned round from the other end of the stall, and Ali smiled in a sickly sort of way.

"What's the matter?" Maya asked, noticing the flushed spots on Izzy's cheeks.

"I was just seeing how my cakes were doing," Ali purred. "Did your mum make any, Maya?"

"No. She's away. 'Scuse me, someone else wants to buy something." Maya hurried back to her place, but she was watching Izzy, and so were Poppy and Emily.

Ali shrugged and wandered away with her friends.

"I think we ought to put a label on her cakes that says Cut-price Bargain Seconds," Izzy whispered to Poppy, wishing she'd thought of it in time to say to Ali – and been brave enough, which she wasn't.

She sighed. Maybe one day.

SIX

Between the cake sale and guessing the weight of the jewelled sponge, the girls had made enough to cover the cost of the skip, but they were still short of the money for the bin bags. But that Friday afternoon, Izzy's dad met her out of school with a huge grin on his face. He was waving a newspaper.

"What is it?" Izzy asked, smiling back even though she didn't know why – she couldn't help it, he looked so pleased.

"This newspaper article! You've solved your bin-bag problem."

Izzy frowned. "The paper! Did they put it in? Show me!"

Her dad held out the paper. It wasn't the front page, but it was still a big piece, with a photo of the girls holding up Maya and Anna's lovely cake, and explaining that they hadn't yet raised enough money to fund the clean-up. There was a photo of the river too, looking a total mess, and Poppy had even managed to get a picture of Billy looking mournful, and holding up his paw (it was actually the wrong one, but no one would ever know). The paper promised that there would be photos of the restored riverside too, if the clean-up went ahead.

"The supermarket rang me – the manager saw the article this morning, and he wants to donate the bin bags to the cause."

"It's us!" Poppy came running up, looking at the photo.

"They should rename that paper the *Park Road Girls News*," a boy from their class said as he walked past. Poppy aimed a half-hearted kick at him.

"We've got bin bags!" Izzy squawked, grabbing Poppy and swinging her round. Then they collapsed into giggles. It sounded such a silly thing to be celebrating.

At last Poppy let go of her. "I'd better go, I can see Mum waving. See you tomorrow! About ten, OK?"

Izzy nodded. The girls were all meeting up at Poppy's house to go and look at the river bank, and make their last plans for the clean-up. She was really looking forward to it.

"Wow," Maya murmured, staring around her. She looked a little daunted.

Izzy nodded, and swallowed. "I was worrying this morning that there might not be enough rubbish to fill a skip, and all these people were going to turn up next weekend, and there'd be hardly anything for them to do…"

Emily shook her head. "Ummm, not so much."

"It's good, really," Poppy said, trying to sound positive. "It means it definitely needs doing. Think how good it will be when it's all tidied up."

"I know." Izzy stared around. "But somehow it looks a lot worse than when we last saw it. I don't remember the bridge being so covered in graffiti before, either."

"It's the rain," Poppy agreed, huddling further into her waterproof and peering out at the drizzle. "It makes everything look worse. Horrible, isn't it? I hope it isn't like this next weekend, that would make it really miserable."

"Uuurrrgh, don't." Emily shivered. "It's supposed to be summer but I'm freezing." Then she jumped as lightning flashed across the dark grey sky over the water. "Oh, no, I hate thunderstorms," she wailed.

"And it's going to tip it down any minute." Maya looked up at the clouds. "Eeek, that was close," she added, as the thunder cracked and growled all round them. "I was going to say let's go back to yours, Poppy, but isn't there anywhere nearer? We're going to get soaked." Fat raindrops were already falling heavily, splashing into the river and pitting the water with little dimples.

"What about under the bridge?" Izzy asked. The rain was getting heavier and heavier, and she didn't fancy legging it back to Poppy's house in this. "Look, there's even a bit of wall sticking out where we can sit down." She led the way along the bank to the bridge, and they huddled underneath, sitting on part of the brickwork that jutted out like a narrow bench.

"It's quite cosy under here," Maya said, pushing back her hood. "No rain's getting in at all."

"And I've just found a packet of mints in my coat pocket," Poppy said happily, handing them round. "Cheer up, Ems, we'll be fine under here."

"If we don't get struck by lightning," Emily said gloomily, shivering as the thunder rumbled around them again.

"We won't!" Poppy put an arm round her. "Don't be so miserable."

Izzy was sucking her mint, and staring out at the sludge-grey water. She looked round at the others worriedly. "I've just had a horrible thought."

"What?" Maya asked anxiously. "Not something else that costs money? I thought we were all sorted."

Izzy shook her head. "No. Look at all that water."

Emily scowled. "We know there's water, that's why it's called a river."

Everyone else ignored her, knowing she was still upset about the thunder.

"What do you mean, Izzy?" Poppy asked.

"It's full of rubbish – not just that bike that Billy got caught in, but loads of other stuff. And lots of it's right out in the middle of the river. How are we ever going to get that out? We won't be able to reach it."

The others looked round at the water. "We didn't think of that," Poppy said slowly. "Oh, rats…"

"However much we clean up the bank, the water's still going to look a mess," Maya sighed.

"We need a boat," Emily muttered. "And no, I haven't got one."

"My dad has," Maya said, without really thinking about it. "But it's in France, so that's no use." Then she blushed, realising she sounded as though she was showing off. "Sorry…"

Emily laughed. "You're so funny."

Poppy squeaked. "Boats! I know where we can get a boat! Well, not a boat exactly, but close."

"You haven't got a boat you've not been telling us about?" Emily asked her disbelievingly.

"No, stupid. But Alex has got a canoe!"

"Ohhhh!" Izzy looked at the water thoughtfully. "A canoe would do, wouldn't it?"

Emily peered out at the rain. "Has Alex said he'll help, then?"

"Nooo…" Poppy admitted.

"Because I can't see him paddling up and down the river all weekend picking up rubbish, somehow."

A smile spread slowly across Poppy's face. "You're totally right," she said happily. "Absolutely right. But he will. Won't he, Izzy?"

"Why? Oh!" Izzy laughed. "Yes, I think he will… You're so mean, Poppy!" But her voice was admiring.

"Have you got something on him?" Emily asked eagerly. "You have, haven't you? Something he wasn't supposed to have done? Something you can threaten to tell your mum about?" She sighed. "Toby and James are always trying to do that to me, but luckily they're useless at it. As if Mum cares that I got ketchup down my skirt. Not much, anyway. Not enough for it to be worth six toffee bonbons, which is what they were asking for."

Izzy and Maya, who were both only children, exchanged "we're so lucky" looks.

"Alex had a date two weekends ago," Poppy said smugly. "A secret date. And then he went out with her again last weekend, and he's supposed to be seeing her today too, to go shopping."

"Why's it so secret?" Maya asked.

"Well, because he doesn't want anyone to know – me and Izzy heard him on the phone. But mostly because the girl he's going out with is somebody my other brother fancies. Alex doesn't want to tell him."

"So you're going to blackmail him into helping us by threatening to tell Jake?" Emily asked.

Poppy nodded. "Yeeees." It did sound a bit mean, now Emily said it like that. She eyed her doubtfully. Was it too horrible a thing to do?

"Excellent." Emily grinned at her.

They hurried back as soon as the rain eased off, although Emily kept flinching every time a car drove past, thinking it was thunder again.

"Mum, is Alex home?" Poppy asked as soon as they got into the house.

"Yes, I think he's in the living room. You poor things, I saw all that rain, you must have been soaked."

"It wasn't too bad, we sat under the bridge," Izzy explained, before Poppy hauled her out of the room.

Alex was lying on the sofa with his phone balanced on his stomach, texting. "What do you want?" he growled at Poppy, looking slightly confused by the line-up of his sister's friends.

"You," Poppy told him sweetly. "You and your canoe. Next weekend."

Alex stared at her. "What for?"

"You know we're doing this big tidy-up of the river," Poppy explained.

"We can't reach the rubbish that's in the water," Izzy told him. "We've just been to see it. There's loads."

"Umm…" Alex seemed to feel a bit embarrassed about telling his sister's friends to get lost, which was obviously what he wanted to do. "That's sad, but—"

"If you don't come and help us, we'll tell Jake about you and Maddy." Poppy smiled even more sweetly.

"You wouldn't!"

"Yes, we would," all the girls chorused.

"You could bring Maddy too – she's got a canoe,

hasn't she?" Poppy suggested slyly. "It might be a fun date."

"I hate you…" Alex growled. "All right. I'll do it."

"Could you ask other people at your canoe club?" Izzy asked him hopefully. "It would be easier if there were more of you. There's quite a lot of stuff in the river…"

"I'll ask," Alex muttered. "Now get lost."

"Bye, Alex!"

"Thanks, Alex!"

"We love you, Alex!"

The girls lay around Poppy's bedroom, their damp clothes steaming gently.

"Is there anything else we have to do?" Maya asked Izzy.

"I don't think so." Izzy had her list in front of her. "Just hope people turn up, I suppose. We have to pick up the gloves and the high-vis vests and the litter-pickers on Friday, but Dad says we can do that after school."

"And the bags are in the boot of my mum's car," Emily volunteered. "So there's no way we can forget them."

Izzy looked at the copy of the poster she had

stapled to the back of her list. *Big River Clean-Up Weekend, Saturday and Sunday, 10 till 4, drop in any time!*

Ten till four. She wrinkled her nose, thoughtfully. What were they going to do afterwards? Perhaps they could go and have tea somewhere – it would be a bit miserable just going straight home. Then her eyes widened, as the vague thoughts turned into an idea.

"Izzy! Your dad's here!" Poppy's mum was calling from downstairs.

"Aww…" Poppy moaned, but Izzy had leaped up and was already dashing for the stairs.

"She's keen!" Emily said, sounding surprised.

"She's left her coat." Poppy picked it up.

"And the list, more importantly," Maya pointed out. "Do you think she's OK?"

Izzy flung her arms round her dad, and he stared down at her in surprise. "What did I do to deserve that, Iz?"

"Well… You haven't actually done it yet…"

"OK. What are you after?" Her dad heaved a huge, exaggerated sigh.

"Can I have a sleepover?"

"A what?" Her dad's face developed a hunted sort of look.

"A sleepover. All four of us, next weekend, on the Saturday, after we've had the first day of the clean-up, because it would be really grim just going home by ourselves afterwards, wouldn't it?"

Her dad didn't look as though he thought it would be grim at all. He looked over at Poppy's mum in a worried way. "Um, I don't know much about sleepovers…"

Poppy's mum rolled her eyes. "They *can* be fun… Poppy has had a couple. I have to say, hers were less trouble than when the boys have them. The mess!"

"Please, Dad! We wouldn't make a mess at all! I promise!"

"What are you talking about?" Poppy asked curiously, as the others came down the stairs.

Izzy looked at her dad with huge, hopeful eyes.

"Oh, all right. I suppose…" he murmured.

Izzy hugged him again. "You really deserve it now!" Then she turned to the others. "Dad says we can have a sleepover on Saturday!"

Her dad sighed. "Hopefully you'll all be really, really tired…"

SEVEN

Izzy woke up on the Saturday morning and leaped out of bed, running to the window to see if it was raining. It had been spitting on and off the previous day, and all four of them had spent most of the time at school staring anxiously out of the classroom windows. They wouldn't call the clean-up off if it was wet, of course, but it wouldn't be nearly as much fun.

She dragged the curtains open hopefully – a greyish sort of day, but no actual rain. That was probably good. If it was too hot, it would be hard to be outside all day, working.

"Izzy!" Her dad was calling her. "Oh, you're awake, that's good. We should have some breakfast and get going."

Izzy scrambled into some old clothes, and took a few minutes to tidy up her bedroom – the others

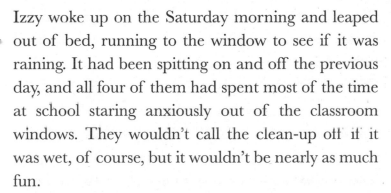

weren't going to sleep there, there wasn't room, but they'd be bound to come upstairs some time and she wanted it to look nice. She'd even vacuumed the carpet the day before, after she'd frantically tidied up downstairs. She'd carefully paced out the space on the living-room floor, and she was pretty sure there was enough room for them all to sleep, providing no one minded squashing up a bit.

She knew it was stupid to be so nervous about a sleepover but she'd never had one before – she'd never been on one, either, so all she knew was what happened in books. She hadn't even had anyone over to her house this whole year at school. So it was reasonable to be a bit nervous, wasn't it? Before her tidying-up spree, she and her dad had spent ages at the supermarket, trying to work out what to get for tea that everyone would like. It took even longer because Izzy insisted on reading the label on absolutely everything – even the biscuits – to check that they were properly vegetarian for Maya. And Fairtrade. And then they had to go back and change the loo rolls for recycled ones.

She looked round anxiously downstairs, and her dad shook his head. "Izzy, it's spotless!"

"How did you know what I was doing?" she asked

– he hadn't even been looking at her, he was making toast.

"Because you haven't stopped worrying about the state of the house, or the fact that the grass needs cutting, or that our wallpaper's a bit old-fashioned, ever since we got home on Saturday. Your friends are coming because they like *you* – not because they're worried that we've got flowery wallpaper in the downstairs loo!"

"I wish we'd painted it," Izzy muttered.

Her dad just sighed. "I suppose if you're stressing about the house and this sleepover, it means at least you're not worrying about the clean-up."

Izzy stared up at him with panicky eyes. "Do you think we need to worry about it?" she asked through a mouthful of toast. She put the rest of the piece down on her plate. She hadn't been very hungry to start with, and now she couldn't eat a thing.

"No! Oh, for goodness' sake, Iz! It's fine. I shouldn't have said anything." Her dad eyed her anxiously. "Cheer up, sweetheart. It's going to be a great day."

"No one's going to turn up, probably," Izzy murmured.

Her dad rolled his eyes and grabbed her plate, emptying the unfinished toast into the bin. "All right.

That's enough. Let's get going now. I can't sit here with you looking like a dead duck any longer."

He swept her out to the truck, which he'd already packed with the bag of high-vis vests and heavy gloves, and the bundles of litter-pickers. They had to drive a slightly different way to the river, as of course they couldn't take the truck through the park. Luckily there was a side road that went fairly close, so the skip could be left there. For anything really heavy, they'd just have to get lots of people to help carry it.

Izzy peered anxiously out of the front window as they arrived in the little road close to the river. "The skip isn't there!"

"Izzy! It's only nine o'clock! It's not due till ten. Calm down, or I'm going to be raving by the end of the day."

"Sorry." Izzy leaned against his shoulder. "I know I'm being stupid. I can't help it. I just keep worrying."

"Mmmm." Her dad shook his head. "Well, stop it. It's going to be fine. It's not raining. And even if no one else turns up, you and me and your friends and their families can still pick up loads of mess. So smile!" He was smiling too, but Izzy could hear a tired note in his voice. She'd been a pain this week, she knew it. Once in a while she had the horrible thought that her dad wished she'd gone with her mum when they split up. It wasn't very often that she thought it – hardly at all, really – but if ever he had, it would be now.

And she was only trying to get everything right, she thought miserably, staring out of the window. It was her idea. She would be the one who got blamed if stuff went wrong.

"What are you looking like a wet weekend for?"

Izzy jumped, nearly throttling herself on her seatbelt.

"Sorry! I didn't mean to make you jump like that, I thought you'd seen me." Poppy eyed her anxiously through the window. "Are you OK? You were looking really miserable."

"She's stressing that no one's going to turn up," Izzy's dad told Poppy, getting out of the truck.

"Well, I'm here, and so's my mum, and my dad's coming later when he's done the supermarket shopping. And Alex is here, and at least six of his mates from the canoe club have promised they're coming." Poppy beamed at her. "So we might get two of them."

"Has he brought his canoe?" Izzy asked worriedly.

"Yes, *of course* he has." Poppy shook her head. "You

really are stressing, aren't you?"

"Come on, you two, help me carry this lot." Izzy's dad handed them each a bundle of litter-pickers, and heaved down the big bag of vests and gloves.

"Excuse me! Are you the ones organising the clean-up?" An elderly lady with a dog was just turning into one of the houses.

Izzy nodded. "Yes," she agreed cautiously, hoping that the lady wasn't going to object about the posters they'd put up, or anything like that.

"Such a good idea! I'll be along later, with my daughter."

"Oh! Thanks!" Izzy beamed, and Poppy nudged her.

"You see! You're just worrying for the sake of it."

✦

Two hours later, Izzy had stopped worrying, simply because she didn't have the time. She was in charge of the sign-up sheets – the lady from the council had explained that they had to get everyone's name and address, just in case anything went wrong – and people just kept on turning up. So far the local paper had sent a photographer, and loads of people had had to pose, beaming, with litter pickers. Four of Alex's friends had arrived – including Maddy, the girl he was secretly going out with, and Poppy's mum had guilt-tripped Jake into helping too, so Alex was trying very hard not to let Jake work out what was going on. Poppy thought it was hysterical, and kept making unhelpful comments just where Jake couldn't quite hear them, to make Alex panic. Izzy thought the photo the photographer had taken of them all lined up in their canoes was going to come out with Alex looking demented, he had such a fixed, panicked grin on his face.

"Hello, Izzy!"

Izzy flinched. She really hadn't been expecting *them* to turn up. She stared at Ali, who was wearing very short shorts and a pair of flimsy sandals that weren't really suitable for scruffing about on the side of a river. Lucy and Elspeth looked pretty much the same – except Elspeth had a floaty skirt on.

"Um, you might get a bit muddy..." Izzy murmured.

"We won't," Ali told her firmly – as if the mud wouldn't dare.

"OK. Well, can you put down your names and addresses, please?"

"Why?" Lucy demanded.

"Er, because that's the way we have to do it. We

have to count people. For Health and Safety."

"That's so stupid," Lucy muttered, and Izzy sighed. No one else had complained. Why was it always these three?

"Hi, Maya!" Ali called, super-sizing her smile and waving madly.

Maya flicked a horrified look at Izzy, who just shrugged.

"Is your mum here?" Ali asked, looking around eagerly.

"No, she's filming in Brazil."

Izzy grinned. Maya had already told them all this, with a furious description of exactly what her mum's flights were doing to the environment. Then she'd sighed and admitted that she wished she was going too – although obviously she wouldn't have wanted to miss the clean-up. It was just that a luxury hotel with a spa and an infinity pool did sound nice. Even if it probably was an ecological disaster. "Mum kept leaving the hotel page open on her laptop," Maya sighed. "It looked gorgeous."

"Oh." Ali was frowning. "I thought she would be."

"Well, she isn't!" Maya snapped back. She was getting really fed up with Ali trying to suck up to her because she was such a little celeb-junkie.

RIVER RESCUE

"Here." Poppy's mum hurriedly slung a high-vis vest round Ali, and shoved a couple more at Lucy and Elspeth. "Come and work on this bit."

Ali looked round, as if she was planning to walk away, but her mum's car was disappearing up the road already. She stomped off in her little gold sandals, twitching at the high-vis vest as if it actually hurt to wear it.

"I really, really hate her!" Maya hissed crossly. Then she sighed. "But I suppose I should have guessed she'd turn up. She's desperate. Do you want a rest from taking the names, Izzy? You've been doing it for ages."

Izzy nodded. "Yes please. I haven't actually touched a bin bag yet."

Maya grinned at her. "I don't think you're missing much…"

"I know, but I'd feel stupid if I didn't do any picking up stuff. Here's the sheets." She passed them over to Maya, and took her gloves and black bin bag in exchange.

The river bank was already looking a bit clearer, but there was definitely going to be more work to be done tomorrow. Alex's friends from the canoe club were picking stuff out of the water, but it was quite tricky – if they tried to pull something heavy, they ended up tipping, and a couple of them had already come close to capsizing. Alex's secret girlfriend, Maddy, had nearly gone in twice, and Alex had been so obviously fussing about her that Jake was now giving him suspicious looks.

Izzy went down to the edge of the water where they'd been piling up the stuff they were dragging out. There was the bike that Billy had got caught up in – or *a* bike, anyway, there looked to be bits of several different ones in the pile.

Alex waved at her, and she waved back, feeling glad that he wasn't in a huff because he'd been blackmailed into helping.

"What are you trying to get out?" she yelled across the water to him.

"Another bike," he called back. "We've done four so far."

"This isn't just a bike," one of his mates said, as he grappled with it. "It's a motorbike. Or half of one, anyway."

Alex shrugged at Izzy. "Where does all this stuff come from?"

Izzy shook her head, smiling, and walked along the edge of the river, stuffing rubbish into her black bag.

It was sunny now, and she'd taken her jumper off. It was lovely feeling the hot sun on her arms. She was daydreaming a bit, imagining her sleepover later. The day was going so well, she'd stopped worrying about everybody hating the tea and being miserable and calling their parents to go home. Now she was imagining Poppy saying it was the best sleepover she'd ever been to, and please could she come to Izzy's house again.

She didn't notice Ali and Elspeth and Lucy, all holding sacks but not actually doing very much, sitting a little further up the bank, and watching her.

"Look!" Alex called to her, and she turned round, right on the edge of the bank, to see what he wanted. "It *is* a motorbike, or bits of it." He was paddling towards her with a wheel balanced on the front of his canoe. "Weird, isn't it? Maybe someone crashed it and threw it in in a strop?" His face changed suddenly and he scowled so angrily that Izzy flinched, wondering what she'd done. "Oi! Don't you dare!"

Izzy teetered on the edge of the water, someone's hand on her arm. For half a second she thought she'd stumbled – it was just too hard to believe that Ali and Elspeth were deliberately trying to push her into the

water. Lucy looked as though she couldn't believe it either – she was hanging back, looking scared. Izzy clawed at the air, trying to save herself, but she was too late. She managed to grab at Ali's high-vis jacket, but it wasn't enough to stop her falling.

Alex shoved the wheel back into the water and paddled furiously towards her, and as she fell, Izzy saw that his friends were heading her way too. *At least there'll be someone to fish me out*, she thought unhappily. *This is so stupid! Everyone's going to laugh at me...*

"Got you!" Alex yelled triumphantly, and Izzy gave a painful little squeak as she hit hard canoe instead of soft(ish) and very very cold water. Only her feet went into the river, and Alex had his arm round her waist, hauling her up. "Sit on the front, that's it."

Izzy shook her head, dazed. The whole thing had happened so fast that she wasn't really sure *what* had happened. There had been such a huge splash. Had her feet really made that much of a splash as she went in?

"Help me!" someone wailed, and Izzy gasped.

It hadn't been her feet at all. It was Ali.

"Why?" Alex leaned over slightly to peer down at her. "You pushed Izzy in, I watched you do it. Stupid little idiot."

RIVER RESCUE

Ali's honey-blonde hair (which Maya swore was dyed, as nobody naturally had hair that colour) was water-dark now, and dripping in rat-tails around her face. She looked furious, and frightened, and somehow a lot less scary than usual. She was splashing about, half-swimming and half-scrabbling at the edge of the bank and Alex's canoe.

Izzy couldn't help it. She laughed. She felt ashamed of herself immediately – Ali could have been hurt, after all. But it was too hard to resist.

"Get me out, it's really deep!"

"Should have thought of that before you decided to push somebody in then, shouldn't you?" Alex growled at her. "I'm not pulling you out. Forget it. Get out yourself."

"What happened?" Izzy's dad, Poppy, her mum, and practically everybody had come running over, and for the first time, Ali started to look alarmed instead of angry. But she wiped the expression off her face after a second.

Emily's dad crouched down and hauled her out, and she stood on the bank shivering and trying to look innocent and forlorn. "Izzy overbalanced, and she grabbed at me and pulled me in after her!" she wailed. Standing there dripping water, with streaks of mud up her legs, and water weed in her pretty sandals, she looked sweetly pathetic.

Izzy gasped. Still, for Ali, it was pretty close to the truth. At least she hadn't accused Izzy of deliberately pushing *her*. Which she could have done, on past history. Then, huddled up on the front of a very wobbly canoe, with her trainers (her old scruffy ones, but still) soaking wet, Izzy lost her temper with Ali. For the first time ever.

"I did not!" she yelled, wriggling out of Alex's helpful arm and letting her dad pull her from the canoe on to the bank. "I didn't fall, and you know it! You pushed me, on purpose!" She was right up in Ali's face, shouting at her. She must have a deathwish, a tiny part of her pointed out, but she squashed it down again.

"Go, Izzy!" Poppy muttered next to her. "Don't let her get away with it."

"She's a little liar! She did push Izzy. I saw," Alex said, loudly and helpfully. "That's why I came in so close, I only just managed to catch Izzy, she wobbled around on the edge for a bit, and I got there just in time."

"I didn't, it was an accident," Ali said hurriedly, stepping back. "You're just clumsy, Izzy." She added

114

something under her breath that sounded like, "And stupid…" and the people around her murmured and tutted, and Izzy's dad took in a sharp breath.

They didn't believe Ali, Izzy realised. They were all staring at her with definite dislike. She'd never seen people do that before. Ali always came out golden, whatever went wrong. Even when Izzy's dad had got her dragged into Mrs Angel's office and accused of bullying, it had somehow ended up being Izzy's fault.

"Are your parents here?" Poppy's mum asked disapprovingly.

"No…" Ali said sulkily.

"Well, we'd better phone them – you need to go home and change."

"And I'll be speaking to your head teacher on Monday morning. This is obviously just more of what's been going on at school," Izzy's dad snapped, pulling Izzy tightly against him as if he thought Ali might try and push her again. "You've been bullying Izzy all year; at least now someone's caught you at it."

"Disgusting," someone behind Izzy muttered.

"Did you swallow any water?" Alex called to Ali, very sweetly.

She stared at him furiously. "What?"

"The water – when you went under, did you swallow any?" He smiled at her. "Or did it get in your eyes, or up your nose?" Some of his canoeing mates sniggered, as though they knew what he was going to say. "Just watch out if you start feeling ill. Like flu? Go to the doctor."

"What are you talking about?" Ali sounded scared now.

"You might have caught Weil's Disease. There's rats round here. You can get Weil's Disease from rat wee."

Ali rubbed her hands on her shorts frantically, as though that was going to help, and sniffed. She obviously had got water up her nose.

"Is that true?" Izzy whispered to Poppy, who was standing right next to her now, glaring at Ali.

Poppy shrugged. "Yeah, I think so, I know Mum watches Alex and Jake like a hawk if they get flu – it looks like flu when it starts off, and they're at risk because of the canoeing. But it's really rare. Super-rare. Just let's not tell Ali that, OK?"

Izzy nodded, smiling to herself.

Poppy's mum led Ali and Elspeth and Lucy up to the side road to wait for Ali's parents. She told Izzy's dad not to get involved, even though he wanted to.

She said he was better off going to Mrs Angel, not getting into a fight now.

Izzy's dad wouldn't let go of her, and he kept thanking Alex for catching her, again and again, so that Alex went bright scarlet and headed further off down the river to get away from it for a bit. Maddy went with him. She was looking very proud of him, Izzy noticed. Poppy and Maya and Emily fussed over her, and Maya lent her a spare pair of wellies that were in Anna's car.

"Let's have our lunch," Poppy's mum said, when she came back. "Those little horrors have gone – I have to admit, Ali's mother did apologise in the end, after she'd said there was no way her little darling pushed someone in the river, and I told her that she'd been caught doing it. Ali was still claiming it was an accident though."

Izzy sat down on the rug that her dad spread out, and nibbled at a sandwich. She felt weird. Shaky, almost. It wasn't from the fall, or she didn't think so. Just surprise, probably, surprise that she'd actually managed to answer back to Ali for once. She still couldn't quite believe she'd said it. People she didn't know kept coming over and asking if she was OK.

"This is really embarrassing," she muttered

eventually, jamming a last chocolate biscuit in her mouth. "I'm going to go and do some more litter-picking, OK?" She was planning to go and tidy up round the bushy bits, where no one would see her.

Poppy and the others scrambled up too. "I know Ali's gone," Poppy murmured, "I just feel like we still need to keep an eye on you! You might end up in the water again."

Izzy sighed, but it was quite nice, really. Especially when Emily kept finding more and more horrible ways to describe what Ali had looked like covered in mud and dripping green slime. It whiled away a long afternoon of picking up crisp packets beautifully.

Izzy had almost forgotten the sleepover, with all the drama. She certainly hadn't worried about it, she realised with a jump, when Emily pointed out that it was two minutes past four and everybody was handing their high-vis vests back to Izzy's dad.

Izzy looked around the river bank. It was a lot tidier – apart from the huge pile of bits of bike and other grot that Alex and his mates had hauled out of the water. They'd have to go and put all that in the skip tomorrow.

"It's starting to look good," Maya said, approvingly. "But there's all that rubbish under the bridge to do tomorrow. And a load of stuff caught up in the bushes on the other side. Do you think Alex could get us over there, Poppy? Sitting on the front like Izzy was? Then we could tidy those bits up too."

"You can't get to it easily from that side," Emily agreed, frowning. "There's that great big wall."

"Don't even think about it," Emily's dad told them. "We don't want any more of you falling in."

Izzy's dad was nodding firmly, and Izzy sighed. It would be really annoying to have one side of the river all beautiful, and the other bank still scuzzy with rubbish.

"Come on, you girls. Help me put this stuff in the truck. Then you can come back to ours." He sighed, and rolled his eyes at Emily's dad. "You can have a cup of tea, and then abandon me with this lot…"

"I'm so full…" Maya moaned.

"I know. It was the chocolate cake." Poppy was stretched out full-length on the sofa. "I don't think I'm ever going to eat again. That was the best cake ever, Izzy. Your dad should open a chocolate cake shop."

"He is good at cakes," Izzy agreed proudly. Her dad had always liked cooking, and even though he

was usually a bit too tired to cook exciting stuff for tea in the week (it was lucky she liked fishfingers, really), he made up for it at weekends.

"I'm getting in my sleeping bag," Emily yawned. "I think I'm caked to death."

"Hey, you lot." Izzy's dad was standing in the doorway, holding the phone, and looking excited.

"No more cake!" Maya yelped. "I'm full!"

He laughed. "You ate it all, anyway. No, I've just had a call from someone at the radio station. How do you girls fancy being on the radio tomorrow morning?"

"Whaaat?" Izzy shrieked.

"They want to interview you, as part of the breakfast show. To try and get more people to come and help, and just because they think you're fab. Someone who helped today rang them up, apparently, and told them it had all been organised by you."

"You helped," Izzy reminded him fairly.

"A bit. But it was mostly you four." He handed the phone to Emily. "You'd better ring all your mums and dads, tell them to listen tomorrow!"

EIGHT

There was a slightly nervous pause, while no one was sure who should talk first. Then Maya jumped in. She wasn't nervous around reporters, she'd been surrounded by them since she was tiny, because of her mum. "It was Izzy's idea," she explained. "She suggested it to us at school a few weeks ago."

"But only because Poppy took me down to the river," Izzy agreed.

"We went for a walk down there with my dog, Billy, and he jumped in the water and got his paw caught up in an old bike that had been dumped there."

"My dad told me that round by the river was really beautiful a few years ago. We even found a sign that said it used to be a nature reserve. So we decided that we'd like to help clean it up," Izzy went on.

"We're just glad it's nice weather, it wouldn't have been as much fun if it was raining," Emily said.

"It definitely wouldn't. And you organised this all by yourselves?" The interviewer's voice was so familiar – Izzy's dad usually put the local radio on when they were on the way to school, and quite often it was Jenny Wells presenting the show.

"It wasn't all that difficult," Izzy said shyly. "We had to get permission from the council, and then we had a cake sale to raise money to hire the skip. Oh! Please can we say thank you to Sampson Skip Hire? They gave us about two-thirds of a skip free! So please use them if you want a skip!"

"And the supermarket in Millford! They gave us all the bin bags," Poppy put in.

"And Mr Finlay and Mrs Angel at Park Road School for helping us with the cake sale," Maya remembered to add. Izzy nodded gratefully. It was a good idea to keep Mrs Angel sweet, and she'd totally forgotten.

Jenny was laughing. "OK, OK. So is there anything else you girls need? The clean-up's going on again today as well, isn't it?"

"Yes. So more people to help would be brilliant," Izzy agreed. "And anyone who can do other things – like maybe make a sign? If we put up a new sign, saying that it's a nature reserve, maybe people wouldn't drop so much rubbish."

"There's a really nice bit under the bridge too, where you can sit and watch the water even if it's raining. If anyone's got an old bench, or something like that, it would be even better…" Emily added.

"Nice idea. And they need to come and find you girls at the river at the bottom of Illroy Park, from ten o'clock today?"

"Yes. And please can we say thank you to everyone who helped yesterday," Izzy added. "There were thirty people altogether, off and on." That was counting Ali, Lucy and Elspeth, who hadn't exactly helped, but thirty sounded like a good number. More of a round number than twenty-seven.

"Of course. So, there you are, everyone. If you've got some free time between ten and four today, get your wellies on and get down to Illroy Park. And a big thank you to Izzy, Poppy, Emily and Maya for such a brilliant campaign."

"We heard it on the radio!" That was what everyone was saying. That and "So which one are you?"

Izzy had told people she was Izzy about fifteen times. But she didn't mind. There were so many of them. And lots of people had brought their own gloves, and even some more bin bags, which was good, because they were starting to run out. The skip was getting full too, and Izzy's dad had done one run to the tip already, with the big stuff, assorted bits of bikes, and the stinky damp mattress. There was a fridge in the back of the truck waiting for the next run.

The best bit was that a man had turned up with an inflatable dinghy in the back of his van, and volunteered to ferry people over to the other side of the river.

"How did you know?" Izzy asked him delightedly. "We were saying yesterday that we couldn't get that bit clean, and wasn't it sad."

He laughed. "I walk my dog along here as well. But I'd never thought of organising everybody to clean it up. Hats off to you girls. Still, I thought to myself that you'd need help getting across to the other bank, so here I am."

She could see them now, a couple of girls from Year Six at Park Road, as well as a few other people she didn't know, filling bags on the other side of the river.

"Do you want a biscuit, Izzy?" Poppy came over with a tin of cookies that her mum had made.

"Hello." An elderly man with a grey, pointed beard was standing in front of her, and Izzy looked back round at him, smiling.

"Hello, have you come to help?" She hoped he would be all right, he looked a little bit fragile for hefting stuff about.

"Yes, although I'm not absolutely sure what you'll want me to do. I heard you on the radio, you see, and one of your friends – at least, I don't think it was you – mentioned the area under the bridge."

"Oh! Do you have a bench you want to get rid of?" Izzy asked him hopefully. No one had turned up offering one yet, but then it had been a long shot.

"No, I'm afraid not. I've come with an idea, instead. I'm an artist, you see. I wondered if we could paint it. The underside of the bridge."

Izzy blinked. "Wow. I suppose we could. Would anyone mind, do you think? What sort of things were you thinking of painting?"

"I'm not sure yet. But I doubt anyone would mind." He smiled. "I've done the same sort of thing before – the council have commissioned me to paint murals in the past – they'll be pleased to get one free, I should think."

Poppy looked at him hopefully. "Would you be

able to paint birds, and butterflies, and that sort of thing? This used to be a nature reserve. Look, just wait a minute." She dashed off, but she was back a minute later with a wooden board with a sheet of plastic over it, very torn and scrappy, and faded by the sun so that most of the pictures on it were a sort of worn-out coffee-brown colour. "You see? It's the old guide to what sort of animals and birds you might see. Herons, look. And water rats. That could be a kingfisher, do you think, Izzy? Your dad said he'd seen one here once, didn't he?"

Izzy nodded. "But what's that got to do with the bridge?"

The old man was nodding excitedly. "You want to do a life-size version!"

"Yes!" Poppy was practically dancing up and down, she was so excited. "It would be brilliant. And I bet there are loads of people here we could ask. People who remember what it used to be like. They could tell us what to paint. Um, that is if you wanted any help?" she added shyly.

"Your idea." The old man nodded at her. "You definitely help. We might not finish it all today, though, if we're doing something complicated like that."

"Oh, I wouldn't mind. Mum would bring me down after school, I bet she would. Or Alex could come and practise canoeing, and bring me with him. That's my brother." She nodded at Alex, who was helping the man with the dinghy heave something disgusting-looking out of the river.

"Right. Well, we need a layer of masonry paint on there first, as a primer." The old man looked suddenly business-like, and somehow much younger. "I brought some, I'll just go and fetch it out of the car. And my acrylics, for the actual painting." He frowned. "Actually, give me quarter of an hour. I'm going to nip to the library, get a few reference books out."

Poppy nodded blissfully, and Izzy laughed. This looked like Poppy's dream come true. As the old man hurried away up the bank, Poppy turned back to Izzy, her eyes sparkling. "This is so cool! This was the best idea ever, Izzy!" She threw her arms round Izzy and gave her a huge hug. "You totally got your own back on Ali yesterday, even if it was by accident. You still told her off, and it was brilliant, and now I get to do some painting with a real artist."

Izzy nodded happily. Poppy was right. And three weeks ago, she thought that Poppy and the others wouldn't want to hang around with her any more. It just showed how wrong you could be.

✦

"Izzy, look!" Poppy was pointing down the river with a paintbrush. She had smears of paint on her nose, and down her jeans, and even in her hair, but Izzy thought she'd never looked happier.

"What is it?" Izzy stood up slowly. Her back was starting to hurt from so much bending over picking up grot, and she was really tired.

"A boat! A beautiful narrowboat, look." Poppy spun her round to see.

"Oh!" Izzy peered down the river. They hadn't seen any boats in the whole weekend, and she certainly hadn't expected to see one. The river had been so full of stuff, a boat as big as that would probably end up with half a washing machine stuck to it somewhere. "Are they stopping?"

"Looks like it to me. Yes, look, that lady's tying a rope to that tree."

"Nice paintwork," George, the artist, said admiringly. "All those flowers."

The boat was beautiful, painted dark green, with curtains at all the windows, and pots of flowers on the roof – it almost looked like a tiny garden up there. And all along the side was the most beautiful painting of flowers. Izzy could just about make out the name of the boat: *Painted Lady*.

Poppy laughed. "We've just done one of those, look! It's a butterfly, this orangey spotted one."

Izzy looked back admiringly at the bridge. It was the middle of Sunday afternoon now, and they'd only just managed to start painting the animals and birds and flowers, because of waiting for the undercoat to dry, but already it was looking beautiful. The butterfly was sitting on top of a clump of painted primroses. Poppy and George had filled in the time waiting for the paint to dry by working out which creatures they would paint, and where, and drawing out life-size sketches that they could transfer on to the wall. It was very organised.

The lady who'd tied up the boat was now walking down the river bank towards them, and the girls smiled at her. Somehow, someone who lived on such a pretty boat had to be nice, they were sure.

"Hello! We heard you on the radio this morning."

Izzy laughed. "Sorry! It's just that so many people have said that today. Your boat's so beautiful. Do you live on it all the time?"

The lady nodded. "Yes – and we often come down

the river here, but we've never been along this bit. Not in the *Lady* anyway, we've walked along, and seen what a state it was in. So when we heard that you were cleaning it out, we thought we might come and help, and then sail on through. I'm Sally. Matt's still on the boat."

"That would be brilliant!" Izzy beamed at her. "Like a grand opening! You ought to have flags!"

Sally laughed. "We have got some, somewhere, from being in a gala day. I'll go and find them, and then I'll come back and do some picking up. Although it looks like you must have nearly finished. It's so much nicer now!"

Izzy nodded. "It's nearly three, and we officially stop at four, so hopefully it's almost done."

"You look exhausted," Sally said sympathetically. Then she smiled. "If you can do without Matt for the last bit of clearing up, I think I'll send him off to the supermarket for some biscuits and stuff. Then we could put the flags up, and you girls and all your helpers could come on the boat and have some tea, and be part of the grand sail-through. A celebration."

"Would you really let us?" Poppy asked delightedly. "It would be a fab end to the weekend. It would have been a bit dismal just giving up and going home."

RIVER RESCUE

"Oh no, you definitely deserve a bit of a party. And now you've cleaned the river up the best way to see how beautiful it is, is obviously by boat." Sally nodded. "Tell everyone, four o'clock, party on the *Painted Lady*! I'll go and make sure she's tidy!"

Izzy sat squashed up in the bow of the narrowboat with Poppy and Maya and Emily, with a glass of lemonade in one hand, and a chocolate biscuit in the other. There was a little bench seat, and there was just about enough room for the four of them, especially as Poppy was kneeling up, and throwing chocolate bourbons to Alex and Maddy and Jake and the others, who were escorting the *Painted Lady* down the river in their canoes. Emily's dad was standing on the bank taking photos, and everybody else was crammed on to the boat, drinking tea, and eating biscuits, and chatting, and generally feeling pleased with themselves.

Poppy's dad had even gone home to fetch more supplies, and Billy too, as he'd helped to start off the whole idea, and now the big dog was happily sitting at Izzy's feet, edging closer and closer to a packet full of bourbons, which Poppy had foolishly left almost in his reach.

"It looks good, doesn't it?" Poppy said proudly, as they sailed under the bridge, and everyone admired the decorated wall. "George says we should finish it in a couple more afternoons."

"It's lovely. It was a fab idea," Maya agreed.

Izzy frowned at the long grasses growing around the edge of the bridge. "Poppy, look!" she cried. "It's one of those butterflies!"

The others stared out across the water.

"There, you see? Just fluttering around those bushes. I'm sure it is one."

"You're right!" Poppy looked delighted. "I know it isn't really because of our clearing up, but it feels like it is! It has to be a good sign, doesn't it? Yay us!"

"Oh, Billy…" Izzy turned to follow the flight of the butterfly as it swooped across the water, and noticed the dog. He glanced up at her guiltily, shreds of biscuit wrapper trailing from between his teeth.

"Not the whole packet?" Poppy sighed.

"And the wrapper, I think," Izzy said worriedly.

"Huh. That won't make much difference, he eats tissues on purpose. His insides are made of iron, the vet said." Poppy shook her head. "Well, I suppose you deserve a treat, since this all started because of you. But you're a bad dog!"

Billy laid his ears flat and whined, and Maya and Emily and Izzy all went, "Awww…" since they weren't as used to his sneaky ways as Poppy was.

Poppy rolled her eyes. "Honestly, he's a thieving horror, and you're feeling sorry for him."

"It *is* a party," Izzy pointed out, scratching Billy under the chin so that he groaned happily. "And it was all because of him, and his silly paws." She giggled. "Maybe we should find some more biscuits, and throw one in the water for that rat he was chasing!"

Billy sat up and stared at her, his bright black eyes sparkling.

"Does he know what rat means?" Izzy asked in surprise.

"Probably. Oh, Billy, no!" Poppy made a grab for his collar, but she was too late. Billy was already gone. He hit the water with a mighty splash, and set about paddling furiously around, clearly hunting the rat that he was convinced must be there somewhere.

"I don't believe it," Poppy muttered. "He's going to have to scramble out on the bank, I'm not going in after him."

"He's a very good swimmer," Izzy said admiringly. Then she smiled, and nudged Poppy. "And at least there can't be any more bikes in there for him to get

133

tangled up in. We carried bits of at least six up to Dad's truck in the end."

Billy seemed to have given up on the imaginary rat now. He paddled hopefully over to Alex and Jake, and scrabbled at the edge of Alex's canoe.

"Poppy!" Alex yelled. "Couldn't you look after the dumb dog for once?"

"Sorry," Poppy shouted back. "He got confused. He went ratting again."

"Typical," Alex muttered, reaching down and hoisting Billy into the cockpit of the kayak in front of him. Billy sat up beautifully, staring ahead down the river, as though he was born to the water. Maddy was paddling along next to Alex, but maybe it didn't matter. Jake's canoe was right up next to the *Painted Lady*, and he was chatting to another girl who'd come to help out. She was lying on the roof next to the flowers, and leaning down to talk to him.

"You know what this means?" Emily said, hopping up suddenly.

The others looked at her in surprise.

"We can open another packet of biscuits, without having to share them with the dog!"

Izzy laughed, and took a bite of biscuit. The sun was definitely hot now, and it really felt like summer.

RIVER RESCUE

It was one of the nicest parties she'd ever been to, Izzy decided. Perhaps it was because they'd been working so hard. Or maybe it was just being on a boat, with all the flags fluttering, and people on the bank waving at them as they floated slowly past. It made her feel like someone really special.

And they were, Izzy realised suddenly, looking at Poppy and Maya and even Emily, all giggling and waving. They were special, all four of them, and she was so, so lucky!

Turn the page for a sneak peek at a
fast paced adventure from Nosy Crow!

A CHASE IN TIME

SALLY NICHOLLS

nosy crow

CHAPTER ONE
THE BOY IN
THE MIRROR

The mirror hung by the stairs in Aunt Joanna's hallway. It was tall and wide, with a gold frame full of curling leaves, and scrolls, and fat baby angels, and baskets of flowers, and twiddles. Aunt Joanna said it had once belonged to a French aristocrat, in the days before the revolutionaries chopped off all the aristocrats' heads and turned their palaces into art galleries.

And once, when Alex Pilgrim was seven years old, he had looked into the mirror and another boy had looked back.

The boy in the mirror was Alex's age, or perhaps a little older. He had light-brown hair and a sturdy sort of face. He was wearing a woolly blue jumper and grey knickerbockers. Knickerbockers, if you don't know, are an old-fashioned type of trouser – shorter than long trousers but longer than shorts – worn by old-fashioned schoolboys in the days before boys were allowed real trousers.

This boy was brushing his hair in the mirror,

rather hurriedly, as though he would much rather be doing something else. As Alex watched, he turned his head sideways and yelled at somebody out of sight. Alex couldn't hear what he said, but it sounded impatient: "I'm doing it!" perhaps, or "I'm coming!" Then he put the hairbrush down and ran out of the frame.

Alex stayed by the mirror. It still showed Aunt Joanna's hallway, but nothing in the hallway was quite as it ought to be. The walls were papered with yellow-and-green-striped wallpaper, and there was a large green plant he had never seen before and a white front door with coloured glass above the sill. It felt very strange not to see his own face looking back at him. He put out a hand,

and there was a sort of ripple in the reflection. When the picture settled, there he was as usual: small, fair-haired, and rather worried-looking. There was the ordinary cream wall behind him. There was the ordinary brown door. Everything just as it always was.

Alex had never believed in those children in books who discovered secret passageways, or Magic Faraway Trees, or aliens at the bottom of the garden, and kept them a secret. Wouldn't you want to tell everyone about them? What was the fun of a secret passage if you had no one to boast about it to?

But he knew that he would never tell his family about the boy in the mirror. Of course he wouldn't.

What would be the point? None of them would ever believe him.

After he saw the boy, though, the mirror became Alex's favourite thing at Applecott House. He liked it more than the long garden with the high stone walls, and the blackberry bushes, and the apple trees. He liked it more than the three cats, and the rabbit in the hutch, and the playroom with the doll's house, and the rocking horse, and the ship in the bottle, and the shelves of old-fashioned children's books.

Alex loved beautiful things. He, his sister Ruby, and their parents lived in a scrubby little house on a scrubby little estate on the edge of an ugly

red-brick town. Aunt Joanna's house was about as different from Alex's house as it was possible for an English house to be. It was big and old and rather grand – it always made Alex think of William's house in the *Just William* books. It had iron gates with a stone ball on the top of each gatepost, and two staircases – a grand one for family and a poky one for the servants. Not that Aunt Joanna had any servants nowadays, of course. Nowadays, she ran a bed-and-breakfast business, and all the bedrooms were kept nice for bed-and-breakfast guests.

Aunt Joanna was really Ruby and Alex's father's aunt. Both of their parents worked busy jobs, which was OK most of the time but made school holidays complicated. Ever since they were small, Ruby and Alex had gone to stay with Aunt Joanna for two weeks on their own every summer. Their parents paid for their bedroom, like proper bed-and-breakfast guests, and every evening they had to write on a piece of paper whether they wanted sausages or eggs or bacon for breakfast. They would help Aunt Joanna with the bed-and-breakfast work as well. Ruby's favourite job was polishing the breakfast table, by sitting on the duster and skidding around on top of it. Alex's was folding the bed sheets, Aunt Joanna on one side, him and Ruby on the other, the three of them coming to meet in the middle.

Applecott House was full of lovely objects. Aunt

Joanna's great-uncle had travelled all around the world collecting things, and most of the things he had collected had ended up in Applecott House. There were jade and ebony cabinets from Japan, statues of gods from ancient Peru, and brightly coloured vases and plates from Turkey. Alex loved them all. But he loved the mirror best.

"Is it very old?" he asked Aunt Joanna, the summer he was ten and Ruby was twelve. "A hundred years old? Five hundred? A thousand?"

"Probably about two hundred and fifty," she said. "It's lovely, isn't it? But I expect it'll have to go when the house is sold."

Because this was the last holiday Alex and Ruby would spend with Aunt Joanna. At the end of the summer, the house was to be sold and most of the lovely objects with it. Aunt Joanna would go and live in a little flat in Eastcombe, by the sea, where there would be no room for beautiful French mirrors or inlaid cabinets from Japan.

Everyone was very sorry about this. Alex minded so much about Applecott House being sold that it hurt. But even he didn't mind as much as Aunt Joanna did. Aunt Joanna had been born in Applecott House. It was Aunt Joanna who had worked so hard to keep it. She had set up the bed-and-breakfast business, and done all the cooking and cleaning and washing and accounting, just so the house didn't have to be sold. But at last, she had had to admit defeat. She was getting too old to do the work. And the house got more expensive to look after every year. Pipes kept bursting, and tiles kept falling off the roof, and mysterious things kept going wrong with the central heating.

"Ah, well," she said to Alex, as he helped to water the garden. "I suppose it had to happen some day. Still, it's a wrench, after all these years."

"I wish I had millions and millions of pounds," Alex said to Ruby that afternoon, as they sat in the garden. Ruby was reading. Alex was playing with a silver bottle he'd found in one of the cabinets. It had a round silver stopper, which he was trying to unscrew, but it didn't want to come out. "I'd buy Applecott House and let Aunt Joanna live here as long as she wanted."

"I wouldn't," said Ruby. "I'd buy a castle in France, with a swimming pool, and a private cinema, and a butler who did everything I asked him to, including homework, and an enormous library like Belle's in *Beauty and the Beast*, and a garden so big I could hold rock festivals in it, and…"

But Alex didn't care about any of those things.

"I want Aunt Joanna not to have to sell the house," he said. "That's all I want."

As he said the words, the stopper came out of the bottle, so suddenly that he dropped the whole thing in surprise. A great quantity of dust and smoke poured out on to his lap.

Ruby said, "Eugh! What is it?"

"I don't know," said Alex. He tipped the bottle upside down, sending another cloud of dust mushrooming out.

Ruby coughed and waved her hands, and said, "I hope that's not something important! What is it, someone's ashes?"

"I don't think so," said Alex. He looked down into the bottle. There didn't seem to be anything else inside. "Not a person's ashes. It might be a hamster's."

"It's old, anyway," said Ruby. She took the bottle from him and frowned. "Yuck! Why don't we ever get a bottle with a genie in it?"

"It'd be my genie if we did," said Alex.

The rest of the day passed the way days at Applecott House always passed. They walked into the village and bought sweets at the Co-op. They picked blackberries from the garden and made a summer pudding for tea. They played a long game of Monopoly that ended, as usual, with Ruby owning half the board, and Alex nothing but two pound notes.

"To buy a cup of tea with," said Ruby. "I'm charitable, me. I give to the homeless."

"Huh," said Alex.

It wasn't until they were going up to bed that he remembered the bottle. There it sat, on the hall table. He picked it up, feeling vaguely guilty.

Perhaps that dust *had* been something important.

"I wish you really were a genie," he said sadly. Then he looked in the mirror, just in case there were any ghosts there tonight.

And there were.

In the mirror were two children. One was the same boy Alex had seen three years ago. Alex had grown, but the boy had stayed exactly the same age, only this time he was wearing a sailor suit and holding a paper bag. An older girl was standing beside him. The girl, who looked about thirteen, had long dark hair and a rabbity sort of face. She was wearing a blue dress, black stockings and a white pinafore. She was trying to take something from the paper bag – Alex guessed it must have sweets in it – and the boy was trying to stop her.

"Ruby," said Alex, very cautiously. "Can you come over here? Like, now?"

"What is it?" said Ruby. Then she looked in the mirror. "*Whoa*."

"You *can* see them," said Alex. He'd been wondering if the whole thing might be a dream.

"Is it projecting from somewhere?" said Ruby. She looked around for a projector, but there wasn't one. "Maybe it's a TV screen," she said. "Is Aunt Joanna doing it? Do you think it's to help sell the house?"

"I don't think it's a TV," said Alex. But he started to feel worried. Could Ruby be right? Could the one magic thing that had ever happened to him be something ordinary after all? "Look," he said, and he touched the glass.

Except that there wasn't any glass any more. His hand went right through the mirror. Ruby squealed.

"Alex!"

Alex tried to pull his arm back, but found that he couldn't. It was like falling downhill in slow motion, except he was falling inside the mirror. He had to step forward to stop himself from tipping over. Ruby said, "Alex!" again, and then, "Alex, what's *happening*?"